THE EULOGY

Book One in the Gift of Grace Trilogy

Debra Yergen

Dear Monique,
You are a lifetime
friend, and I am so
truly thankful for you.
♡ debra

Whole House Publications
S·E·A·T·T·L·E

Dedicated to my families – the one I was born into and friends who have become family along the way.

A special dedication to my mom, Sandi, whose love truly inspired this tale.

Library of Congress. First Edition.

ISBN: 9781092424677

We hope you enjoy this book from Whole House Publications.

www.WholeHousePubs.com

Printed in the United States of America.

ACCEPTANCE ▪ TRANSFORMATION ▪ TRUST

Book I: *The Eulogy*, begins a story about acceptance
and the journey to like the ones we love.

Book II: *The Bench*, deals with transformation and the pas-
sage to reclaim the dreams we know are possible.

Book III: *The Gathering*, brings home the   import-
ance of trust and the way we learn, live, and offer generous help-
ings of forgiveness to ourselves and those who share our path.

Join the fan conversation.

https://www.facebook.com/YergenTrilogy/

CHAPTER 1

The chilly October afternoon Isabelle rushed to Providence Portland was not exceptional, aside from the fact that she didn't know what to expect when she arrived. Usually her chaos was predictable. But not today. Her brother, Zach, hadn't really given her any information, other than that she needed to come quickly. In fact, he hadn't even given her a room number, and in her haste, she forgot to ask.

When she arrived at the hospital, the line to guest services was four deep, so instead of stopping, she walked briskly past the desk, toward the elevators, and dialed the hospital operator from her cell. Before the attendant completed her formal greeting, Isabelle interrupted, asking to be connected to Harriet Zelner's room. *Please pick up. Please pick up.* Isabelle recognized her brother Zach's voice, and asked the room number. She was already in the elevator when he told her ICU-12, and after glancing at the floor map in the elevator, she reached over and pushed the button for the second floor. It was by coincidence she had selected the green elevators. She knew the intensive care unit signaled the seriousness of Harriet's condition.

Once she arrived at the intensive care unit, Isabelle paused to compose herself before walking into her aunt's room. Even collected, she appeared somewhat disheveled with her hair pulled back, a bag over one shoulder and her purse in the other hand. She knew she needed to downsize her daily luggage, but that would require her to plan ahead as to what she might actually need in any given day, and it was so much easier just to carry everything with her.

Her eyes immediately focused on the frail woman in the bed. It shocked her to see her aunt this way given the conviction of Harriet's normally confident disposition as Zach and Isabelle were growing up. It felt surreal seeing her hooked up to so many wires and tubes. Harriet had been hospitalized before, but this stay in the ICU brought with it a more ominous feel.

"I'm glad you could make it," Zach said.

"I rushed to get here," Isabelle retorted.

"Must have been a lot of red lights," Zach said.

Isabelle didn't respond. She knew it did no good to engage him when he was like this. He wasn't always so sardonic, so consistently surly, but he had become more so over the years, and Isabelle had learned how quickly innocent banter could turn into an all out family war.

Standing bed-side, Isabelle leaned down and kissed their aunt on her forehead. "She looks so peaceful," she observed.

"Too bad it took this." Zach snickered. "Hey, what's that smell?"

"What smell?"

"You smell like raw fish," Zach said. The normally unaware man walked determinedly toward his sister, repeatedly sniffing the air and mercilessly teasing her as he got closer.

"What are you talking about?" Isabelle was visibly annoyed that the only interest her brother seemed to take in her was to poke fun at her admittedly unusual smelling new face cream. She swatted at the air to send him a message to leave her alone.

Zach got right up to Isabelle's cheek and neck area and

coughed. "Is creamed herring the new health fad you recently signed up to try?"

"Stop it. Leave me alone," Isabelle snapped her hand at Zach's leg. "It's different, but it's not terrible."

"Oh it's divine – if you're an alley cat." Zach laughed.

Isabelle wrinkled her nose. *It's not that bad.* To be honest, she had the same reaction in her bathroom at home when she first opened the box, but she assumed it was the concentration of it in the bottle and that the smell would dissipate. *Guess I'll be throwing this stuff away.* She frowned. She couldn't return it as she bought it in an airport the last time she was traveling home on a business trip.

Interrupting the sibling spat, a nurse with hot pink tubing on her stethoscope walked into the room with a vitals cart. "I like your bling," Isabelle said.

"Thanks. We have fun with pink in October." The tiny nurse with matching pigtails and long, dark eyelashes smiled. Isabelle didn't readily connect, nor did the nurse explain, that October was breast cancer awareness month, widely supported by pink ribbons and other accessories. Isabelle was still stuck on the fact that her brother thought she smelled like sour fish. It chipped away at her confidence. *I hope the nurse can't smell my face cream.*

The nurses and physical therapists visited Harriet every couple of hours, which gave Isabelle the sense that her medical team was doing everything possible to give her aunt a fighting chance. Zach was on his best behavior when he and Isabelle weren't alone to pick at each other.

As Harriet's only surviving family members, Zach and Isabelle had been briefed on the immediacy of Harriet's condition. Their aunt had suffered a hemorrhagic stroke. Despite a team of intensivists, neurologists, internists, physical therapists, respiratory therapists and of course the always kind nurses who never treated their questions like an inconvenience, the biggest take-away for Zach and Isabelle was that the prognosis for Harriet's survival sat at only twenty-five percent. Thankfully, one of their close family friends was an emergency physician at this same hospital. Carrie had been a great support to Zach and Isabelle throughout Harriet's hospitalizations over the years, and she offered them both answers and a bit of hope. Isabelle was confident that if anyone could survive this it would be Harriet, but Zach was not so certain.

Isabelle mildly resented Carrie's constant presence in their lives, despite the fact that she couldn't put her finger on why. Carrie was eight months older than Isabelle, but she might as well have been years ahead based on her many achievements and regular investments in humanity, all of which Harriet proudly and frequently shared with Zach and Isabelle over the years.

Unlike his sister, Zach was completely detached from any of what he coined *chick shit.* He wasn't the least bit aware of Isabelle's feelings of competition and insecurity toward Carrie. In fact, he was completely oblivious even to the tension between his sister and his aunt. Zach operated from the fifty thousand foot perspective of life, *describing himself as a big picture guy*. He was a man driven to extremes by everything from his penchant for risk to his multifarious moods and wry sense of humor.

"How's she doing?" Isabelle asked the nurse.

As the nurse started to respond, Isabelle's face fell as she realized she completely forgot to pick up her daughter from ballet. She checked her phone, which was on vibrate in her purse, and saw there were three missed calls. The ballet class had been over for an hour. She didn't want to interrupt but she suddenly felt pulled between being rude and getting to her child.

Just then, Zach's girlfriend-of-the-month walked in, glamorous, self-assured and aloof. *Yet another example of his penchant for ephemeral perfection.* Zach didn't make any observations about her being late. Isabelle tried to ignore her legs that seemed to go on for miles in her mini skirt designed for someone fifteen years younger. Isabelle wondered how she was allowed access to the ICU, but knew that even asking the question would likely lead to a place she didn't want to go. And so Isabelle waved politely to Amone, a gesture which went completely unacknowledged by both Amone and her brother. Amone either didn't notice or didn't care to respond, but instead walked over to Zach and draped herself all over him, ignoring Isabelle and the nurse. And Aunt Harriet.

The nurse with the brightly colored stethoscope barely seemed to notice Amone's grand entrance, but Isabelle did. Without missing a beat, the nurse noted that the intensivist would make rounds in the next hour if they had additional questions. Isabelle had so many questions but they would have to wait.

When the nurse left the room, Isabelle picked up her purse and clunky bag before apologizing for running out so quickly, explaining that she forgot to pick up Grace at ballet.

"Good thing you misplaced that application for mother of the year award," Zach joked and then laughed. Isabelle clenched her fist and hurried out without responding. "It's a joke, Izz. It would do you good to learn to laugh," he called out as she exited the hospital room. Isabelle refused to acknowledge what she considered to be his juvenile humor.

On the way out, Isabelle began texting the other parents, hoping one of them would write back that Grace had caught a ride with them. No one immediately responded, leaving Isabelle feeling simultaneously scared, worried and frustrated.

In her state of frustration and haste, Isabelle didn't notice a soda that had been dropped on the floor just outside of the elevator, until she stepped in the small puddle, leaving the bright red soles of her shoes sticky from the syrup. She didn't notice the grieving family in the first floor hall that she had to step through on her journey to the entrance. She didn't notice the doctors and nurses running toward her, and then past her to the elevators. She didn't notice the Code Blue called overhead.

All she could think of was getting to her car and to her daughter – hoping the school was still open or that someone could tell her if her daughter had gone home with a friend. Isabelle's spirit was crushed by Zach's thoughtless remark about her not being mother of the year. She knew she wasn't mother or anything else of the year, but she wanted to be. Deep down she wanted to be someone else – or at least a brighter, sunnier, better organized version of herself.

Zach always knew how to hit her where it hurt.

When she arrived at the rustic, brick building that housed the ballet school, it was dark. The lights were out and the doors were locked. She called out for Grace but Grace wasn't there. Panic strangled her. Her breathing was staccato and she began to cry. In her gut, she knew her daughter was safe. But where was she? And what must whoever had her be thinking about Isabelle? She placed the last call she wanted to make – first. She called Arnie – her estranged husband and father to Grace – although a much better father than husband at this point.

"Grace is missing," she started. Arnie let her talk. In fact, he let her tell her entire panicked story, so soon she was sobbing and repeating, "I'm sorry. I'm so sorry."

It was only then that he volunteered the news she wished he would have said when he answered. "I have Grace. She's fine." Isabelle was at the same time relieved and angry. It was just like him to let her go on and on like that when he could have immediately put her mind and fears to rest.

When Isabelle arrived home, she flung open the door from the garage, which led to the pantry next to the kitchen. Without bothering to shut the door completely, she ran through the pantry, nearly tripping on some shoes. When she reached the kitchen, she found Grace sitting calmly and completely content at the kitchen counter in a yellow t-shirt, denim shorts and bare feet. Her crayons were spread across the counter, and a few had rolled off onto the floor. She was drawing a picture of a mom, dad, child, sunshine and grass. Isabelle didn't bother to remove her coat before rushing to her child.

Grace's pictures always included sunshine and grass. Isabelle found this both mystifying and at the same time oddly comforting. Isabelle appreciated the stability Grace's childish drawing represented, but unfortunately it did not represent the reality of their lives. Isabelle hugged Grace and exhaled slowly. "I'm so sorry, baby," she said.

"It's ok, mom. Dad said you forget a lot of things and not to take it personally," the eight-year-old reiterated the explanation she had received an hour or so before.

"I do have a lot going on, but I never forget you," Isabelle explained.

"It's ok. I'm fine," Grace said.

"Honey, I didn't forget you. I was at the hospital with Yia Yia and I tried to get away. She's very sick. I'm sorry," Isabelle insisted, seething that Arnie would actually tell Grace something like that. *It was just like him to be so insensitive.* Isabelle did not see herself as a walking mess of a mother. She saw herself as a woman over-committed and under-equipped with the resources to please all the people who mattered so much to her.

Even when she was frustrated with Arnie, she never shared her misgivings with their daughter, and it more than pained her, it infuriated her that he didn't extend her the same courtesy. Of course, Arnie had a very different perspective. He considered his comments harmless. He certainly didn't intend to cause the enormous disruptions that always seemed to occur when he offered up what he considered to be the smallest joke about her less than stellar juggling abilities as of late. And frankly, the fact that Isabelle had the same issues with Arnie as she also had with Zach only further supported Arnie's belief that Isabelle was the one with unresolved issues and hyper sensitivities.

Arnie was leaned back in the recliner watching football in the den with a bag of potato chips in his lap when Isabelle walked in. "Really, Arnie?" she started. He looked up at her surprised. "You told Grace I forget things?" Isabelle fumed.

"Hello," Arnie said, pausing a beat for effect. "Thank you. Those are things you might say to someone who picked up your daughter, brought her home, fed her dinner, and babyset her until you were able to arrive," Arnie said.

"And that's the problem," Isabelle pointed out. "You are not her babysitter. You are her father. Picking her up does not make you a superhero. And," now she paused for effect, "you told her I can't remember anything, so now she thinks I'm unreliable." Isabelle was so irritated she forgot she hadn't said thank you, until he mentioned it, and now she didn't feel like saying thank you, even if she had remembered.

Isabelle and Arnie's relationship started out with what seemed like such perfection compared to how it had deteriorated over the years. He was a fun and romantic boyfriend – playfully making jokes, surprising her with adventures, and encouraging that reluctant seed of spontaneity in her to sprout. There was a time he practically took her to Disneyland every time they went to bed! Unfortunately, the things she loved about her boyfriend became the same things that failed her in a husband who she expected to protect her from life's complications and adjust to the responsibilities of parenthood the way she thought he should. It wasn't so much who he had become that bothered her, as much as who she had become in response to their changing lives and roles.

She had become the protector and the guardian of their security, and instead of stepping up and taking charge, he criticized her initiative to oversee a job she never wanted in the first place.

"She's a smart kid, Izz. She's got this figured out," Arnie snipped. *Those are fighting words*. She was never happier that he had moved out than she felt in that one moment. She was tired and had become frequently irritated at his blanket observations and insults.

"Why didn't you call me to let me know you had her? Why did you let me frantically scramble to find her?" Isabelle fired back in a high-pitched tone. Arnie hated it when she whined. It was his equivalent of nails on a chalkboard, and he didn't want to be there anymore than Isabelle wanted him there.

Arnie stood up to leave and turned to Isabelle. "I'm sorry for whatever your current crisis is, but it would have been really nice if you could have just said, 'thank you,'" he stated mater-of-fact as he picked up his jacket.

"Thank you," Isabelle said, before pausing. "Thank you for picking her up. You're right. I should have said that first." If only she had stopped there, her acknowledgement would have made a difference to Arnie. He still loved the girl he fell in love with more than a decade ago. But Isabelle could never just stop. It wasn't in her nature to let things lie. She always had to defend herself, and offer one more excuse or far more explanation than the situation required, which more often than not completely reversed her minor efforts to get along.

"Harriet is in the hospital again. She had a stroke. She may die. But I didn't know that much when Zach called and said it was an emergency. I rushed there and I guess I lost track of everything else for that tiny piece of time while I was responding to my current crisis. And I'm sorry that inconveniencing you pissed you off so much that you had to punish me. But I'm not unreliable, and how dare you perpetuate that myth, originally or secondhand to our daughter," she said more softly.

Arnie stood before her expressionless, looking at her with what she frequently referenced as his blank stare. She couldn't read his mind. She couldn't even read his face. While Arnie was drawn to Isabelle's passion and exuberance for life, over time her constant nagging and inability to simply do things his way occasionally, made their relationship increasingly miserable for him. He didn't want her to lose her personality – simply to compromise some of the time.

The truth was that Arnie was in many ways unconventional, but not to the point of putting the well-being and security of his family at risk – a concern Isabelle never outright articulated, but too often hinted. He desperately wanted to give Isabelle and Grace a better life and he believed that would require both creativity and risk on his part.

Finally, he moved to turn away.

"It's ok. She's fine. And I did call you. I must have called your work number. I left a message. I wasn't trying to freak you out but," Arnie stopped after "but" and changed direction with what he was going to say. "I was going to ask you if you wanted me to move back in, to try one more time to make this work, but after tonight, I think it's probably good that we take some time apart right now. I'm sorry your aunt is sick. And Grace is ok. She is ok, Izz. I made her dinner. Hug her. Put her to bed. We have a great kid. We did that right at least. I gotta go," he said as he turned back and leaned in to kiss Isabelle on the forehead, before he stepped back away and headed toward the door. She wanted to push him away when he kissed her, but she didn't. *Why does he always have to be so stupidly patronizing?*

When Isabelle walked into the kitchen, Grace was just finishing her drawing. She had added a house and a dog. Her big hazel-colored eyes looked sad. Isabelle knew she must have heard them fighting in the other room. *Do I address this or let it go?*

"I see you're still holding out for that dog," Isabelle said as she picked up Grace's drawing and carefully looked it over. "This is really good, honey." It pained her that Grace's pictures always included the three of them. Even more, she worried that Grace remained steadfast in believing that their little family would remain intact, when in fact, this was a reality about which even Isabelle could no longer be sure. She wanted to bring it up, but she was afraid of what Arnie may have told their child, and she didn't want to initiate a difficult conversation before bed. Isabelle wasn't emotionally capable of witnessing, let alone responding to, anyone else's tears that night – especially her daughter's. She knew there were no easy answers.

The reality was that Arnie was not moving back into the house. The divide between them was too wide to bridge right now and Isabelle had more pressing matters on her mind. She sat down next to her daughter and said the words she had always longed to hear in her own small ears decades before. "Grace, I made a mistake tonight. I was at the hospital. I forgot to make arrangements to have dad pick you up and I'm sorry. I'm glad he was there. You must have been really scared." Isabelle didn't like admitting her mistakes.

The little girl took it all in stride, "It's ok, mommy."

"It's not ok, and it won't happen again. I love you, Gracie," Isabelle cradled the little girl she loved so much.

"I love you too, mommy," Grace said.

"What do you say we get your bath going?"

Grace wrinkled her nose. "Do I have to wash my hair?" Grace pleaded against it, shaking her little head no and scrunching her face.

"You don't want to stink," Isabelle said, playfully holding her nose and mimicking Grace's expression. Suddenly, Isabelle remembered how she felt in the hospital when Zach made fun of her face cream. She didn't want to make Grace feel this same humiliation. Grace pouted and made groaning sounds, which cued Isabelle to quickly give in a bit. "You don't have to wash your hair tonight but you need a bath," Isabelle said. Grace agreed and walked out of the room and down the hall sliding her feet in a shuffle along the wood floor.

Isabelle reached down and unzipped her camel-colored boots. She peeled off her socks and tucked them into her boots before sitting back down on a stool at the kitchen bar.

Isabelle laid her head on her folded arms on the kitchen counter. *How has this become my life?* Nowhere in her planning had Arnie moved out or Zach become such a jerk with all his *master of the obvious* observations. They were both monumental disappointments. *What if everything in her life were different? What if she had never broken up with the Portuguese exchange student she fell madly in love with in college? What if she had followed Masingho back to Europe and had never met Arnie or even moved to San Francisco? What if she had become a novelist like she once planned instead of managing large third-party insurance brokers?* She wouldn't have Grace. That wasn't a thought she wanted to entertain for even one second.

Just as she started to feel lost in a daydream, she suddenly looked up when she heard heels clicking behind her, on the floor across the room. Someone was in her house, with her and her daughter – someone she had not invited in. *Arnie must have left the garage door up when he left.*

She looked at the counter for what she could grab to defend herself, but all she saw were a couple of magazines and a ketchup bottle Arnie had left out. "Stop there!" she warned, with her back still toward the intruder. She hadn't considered if the prowler was armed. She didn't have time to plan a response if the shadow in her kitchen had shot back, "Or what?" Or worse, what if she heard the snapping sound of a cocking gun?

Fear was not an option. She had her child to protect. Pulling together every ounce of courage and confidence she could muster, she spun around swiftly, never expecting to have her breath grabbed from her chest as she exhaled with force and froze.

Isabelle began to panic. She covered her mouth. She couldn't even blink at first. All she could do was push out and inhale tiny breaths of air. *Where was her phone? Who would she call? There's no way this was really happening.*

Not again. No, not again please. Isabelle gasped for air, the way she first had several months ago when she was sure she had developed an arrhythmia, only it turned out to be a panic attack. The first time was her worst – it lasted five days. In stressful circumstances since, she had moments of relapse, but nothing like the first time.

Her first symptoms back in June, when Arnie moved out, started with an entire weekend of continual yawning. This led to yawning followed by needing to take one deep breath after another, like on mornings when she woke up without having slept enough. Only one deep breath wouldn't be enough. As soon as she caught her breath, she would yawn again and need to take another breath.

Even just thinking back to that time intensified her symptoms. She actively had to force herself to not think about that and instead repeat what Carrie had told her. *You do not need to gulp in these huge breaths of air. Your saturation levels are fine.* It was a reminder that normally helped her, despite the fact that prior to these episodes she didn't even know what oxygen saturation levels were.

And sure enough, just as instantly as she became aware of the intruder, the early symptoms of the panic attack started. Those familiar yawns followed by her slow gasps for deep breaths of air commenced. Isabelle's chest was tight and her heart raced. There were few things she hated as much as these episodes.

Isabelle had become accustomed to talking herself into believing or not believing things that made life easier for her to accept. She did this with strangers. She did this with friends.

She also told herself a lot of things about Arnie. And Zach. And Harriet. *Harriet's advice is intended to help me be a better person. Harriet loves me the way I am. Harriet appreciates all I do to help her.* It would have been impossible for her to make the sacrifices she made on a regular basis if she didn't convince herself that they were quietly recognized and appreciated by the people who meant so much to her, even if none of them actually verbalized their appreciation with words of affirmation.

Isabelle struggled to come to terms with what her eyes were telling her. She struggled to differentiate if it was real or in her mind. *Is this a dream?*

The woman in her house was not a stranger, and yet, she certainly didn't belong there. Not now. Isabelle bit her lower lip the way she always did when she was scared or angry. *What in the hell?*

It was Harriet.

The intruder was Harriet. Aunt Harriet, in the hospital. Only she was here – in Isabelle's kitchen. And she was twenty-five years younger than her current version lying in a hospital bed across town. The wrinkles in her cheeks and forehead were gone. Her hair was dark again, not gray. The hollows in her cheeks were filled out as they were in her youth. It was Harriet, but it wasn't Harriet. It was how Isabelle remembered Harriet, which is what made her question everything about the interaction. There was no way she could easily accept something so spooky. It just didn't make sense.

Isabelle shook her head and blinked.

I must have fallen asleep. Or maybe I'm going crazy.

She cautiously stepped closer until she was face to face

with Harriet, who was almost her same height. They were eye to eye, Harriet in heels and Isabelle barefoot. Isabelle examined her aunt, looking her up and down as Harriet had done so many times with Isabelle.

Isabelle blurted out, "Did you die?"

"No one told me if I did," Harriet said.

"Well, I left you in the hospital, a few hours ago, and," Isabelle put her hands on her face as her eyes grew wide. "Oh my gosh, the Code Blue. I didn't even think about it but, yes there was a Code Blue. I was in a hurry to, uh. Was it you?" Isabelle asked, jumbling her words together in rambling nonsensical sentences.

Had she finally lost her mind? Had her aunt passed away and come to her now, somehow years younger, which seemed weird but oddly comforting? Was she dreaming? Had she fallen asleep? Isabelle was pretty sure Harriet wasn't an angel, but then, maybe she was. Was this a terrible joke orchestrated by Zach? And if their aunt had died, wouldn't Zach have called? Wouldn't someone have called? "Who sent you?" Isabelle asked. "Why are you here?"

Harriet simply smiled. Her eyes were warm. "I'm here because you need me," Harriet said. "I've always been here when you've needed me." Isabelle could think of more than a few times when she needed Harriet and she wasn't there, but this didn't seem like the time to bring all that up. "You weren't really very nice to Arnie. Is it really any surprise he left you?" the younger version of the same old aunt chimed in.

Seriously? Same opinionated Harriet. Isabelle broke her stance and walked away abruptly, headed toward the door. "I'm not going to fight with you and I don't need you here," Isabelle said. The moment she said that she wanted to take it back.

Inside she was torn. If her aunt had died, this might be her last time to see her, to talk to her, to thank her for all she really had done. Despite her rough edges, Harriet and Uncle Frank took Zach and Isabelle in as their own children when their parents were killed in a car accident. If it hadn't been for them, the two may have been separated or bounced from one foster home to the next. Instead, they grew up in a well-appointed home – where they were loved and given every material advantage in life. *It's hard enough losing your parents at such a young age.* Despite what a jerk Zach had become over the past two decades, as children, he was highly protective of his little sister. Isabelle couldn't imagine growing up without any of them – Zach, Harriet or late Uncle Frank.

When Isabelle was Grace's age, Harriet adored her. She fussed over her continuously. She dressed her fashionably and paraded her to the many organizations to which she volunteered her time and talents. But as Isabelle got older, into her teen years, the two began to argue incessantly. Nothing Isabelle did seemed to meet the impossible standards set for her by Harriet.

Isabelle suddenly remembered Grace – taking a bath and getting ready for bed. She looked at the clock and saw that Grace had been gone for fifteen minutes. *She should be drying off by now.*

"I need to check on Grace," Isabelle announced.

Just then, Grace appeared in the kitchen in her fluffy pink bathrobe. "I'm right here."

Could Grace see Harriet too? How would this be for her? Should Isabelle acknowledge their guest or just hope she was invisible – not to mention silent? When was Harriet ever silent? In the hospital – Harriet was silent in the hospital – on a ventilator with a feeding tube. Oh that was a horrible thought. Isabelle cringed. "How was your bath?" Isabelle asked.

"It was a bath. I'm hungry. Can I have cereal?" Grace asked. Grace didn't appear to notice anything out of the ordinary.

"May I..." Harriet corrected the child.

Isabelle looked back and forth between Grace and Harriet. Isabelle coughed a bit as if she had swallowed air. She was nervous about so many things. This whole experience was so far outside of her comfort zone, and she didn't feel even a little bit comfortable acknowledging it to herself, let alone probing to discover if Harriet was visible to Grace as well.

"May I have cereal?" Grace rephrased the question. Isabelle was speechless. *Wouldn't Grace say something if she saw Harriet? She doesn't seem scared.*

"Didn't daddy feed you dinner?" Isabelle asked, trying to act normal, but still coughing.

"Yes, but I'm hungry," Grace replied. "Are you okay?"

Whoa! That was a question Isabelle didn't know how to answer. So she sidestepped it. "You can have a little cereal before you go to bed, but not the sugary ones." Isabelle reached for the corn flakes. She knew they weren't Grace's favorite, so if she was really hungry she'd eat them and if she wasn't she'd push them away. Grace sat at the counter and Harriet sat beside her while the child ate four or five bites before pushing the bowl away. "Okay kiddo, time for bed. Brush your teeth and I'll be down to tuck you in." Again, Grace shuffled away.

"So what are we going to do about you and Arnie?" Harriet asked when Grace left the room.

"We aren't going to do anything," Isabelle said, stressing the word *we*.

"What are you going to do about Arnie?" Harriet restated.

"Look, I don't know why you came or how long you'll be here, or if you're even here at all, but whatever time you are here, I don't want to spend it talking about my failing marriage to Arnie," Isabelle said.

"What do you want to spend it talking about?" Harriet

asked.

"I don't know. I guess I want to know why you're here and what I'm supposed to do about it," Isabelle said.

"Well, that's up to you," Harriet said. "I love you, Isabelle. I've always loved you."

Oh my gosh, you are dead. "I love you too, Harriet. That was never in question," Isabelle sighed and shook her head. "I need to put Grace to bed. I'll be back in a few." Isabelle wasn't sure what was going on – with anything in her life, frankly. How had it spun so far out of control?

Grace was in bed asleep when Isabelle walked into her room. Isabelle pulled the covers up, and Grace awoke for a few seconds, long enough to say, "Good night, Mommy. Good night Yia Yia," before turning on her side and falling back asleep.

Yia Yia was Grace's name for Harriet. Isabelle had no idea where it came from. It was Greek for grandmother but Grace had never been to Greece. *Could Grace see Harriet? Was she real? Was she here? Did she die tonight and no one called to let me know?* She didn't want to wake Grace up to get to the bottom of this now.

When Isabelle walked back into the kitchen to finish her conversation with Harriet, her aunt was nowhere to be seen. "Harriet?" Isabelle called. No answer. No presence. No Harriet. Just then the phone rang.

CHAPTER 2

I t was Zach. He was calling to say he just left the hospital and there was no change with Harriet. According to Zach, a neurologist stopped by to let the family know he had ordered a CT which would tell them if she had significant cerebral edema.

Isabelle didn't know what that meant so she jotted it down on a napkin so she could text Carrie about it when she hung up the phone. Carrie's mom and Harriet had served on several Portland boards together before she passed away. Harriet had taken Carrie, an only child, under her wing like a surrogate daughter – just has she had done with her nephew and niece so many years ago. On the phone, Isabelle didn't want to admit to Zach that she didn't recognize the medical terminology that later seemed like a fancy way of saying swelling around the brain hemorrhage.

Zach let Isabelle know that Harriet's blood pressure had already come down to a safe level, but he said she would need to remain on the ventilator for now. They would know tomorrow if she needed surgery or if the medicine alone would pull enough of the fluid off her brain into her bloodstream, lowering the intracranial pressure. At seventy, she wasn't old by medical standards, but she wasn't of an age where doctors considered her highly resilient either.

"So she's alive?" Isabelle asked.

"Harriet? Yeah." Zach asked and answered without pausing for confirmation. So Isabelle hadn't been visited by a ghost – or an angel, which she had already surmised. "Did you find Grace?" Zach inquired.

"Arnie picked her up. He left a message on my work phone while I was at the hospital, so I basically freaked out and probably didn't seem at all grateful for him picking her up and taking her home."

"At least she's okay. You, you gotta relax, Izz. You're wound so tight you're gonna have a stroke if you're not careful." Zach extended about as much support as he was capable of extending. She could tell by his tone he was making an effort, so she also took a pause, trying not to let him hear her struggle for cooperation.

"I'm not going to be at the hospital tomorrow. I have a conference in San Francisco. I'll be back Thursday night," Isabelle informed him. She didn't know why she was telling her brother this. She supposed it was because she needed to tell someone. Wednesday nights were Arnie's, so it seemed unnecessary to tell him her every move anymore, given their separation. Now, Zach was all she had.

"Have a safe trip," Zach said.

"You'll let me know if there are any changes with Harriet?" Isabelle asked. Zach confirmed he would.

Isabelle texted Carrie, an ER physician, who was always prompt with her responses, especially where Harriet was concerned. Isabelle was glad Harriet had Carrie to watch out for her. A tiny part of her wished she had such a warm and amiable relationship with her aunt. Harriet never seemed to impose her opinions on Carrie the way she so naturally did with Isabelle. Either that or it didn't bother Carrie the same way. Carrie often referred to herself as "Harriet's other daughter," which Isabelle mostly accepted to mean the sister she never had.

In addition to explaining the tests Harriet would face the next day, Carrie put Isabelle's mind at ease by sharing with her that Providence Portland offered some of the best imaging diagnostics on the West Coast, and even the nation. Isabelle knew her aunt was in the best hands possible and that helped to calm the worries running circles in her mind.

When Isabelle crawled into bed, she lied there, on her back, eyes wide open. She noticed how bright it was and got up to discover a full moon outside. She rarely looked at the moon or noticed what went on in the sky or even in nature. If there wasn't a calendar in every room of the house, open to October, she couldn't have told anyone it was even fall. It's not that she was self-absorbed. She just failed to pay attention where it mattered most – and paid too much attention to things she would have been better served to let go.

◆ ◆ ◆

It was raining when the plane touched down in San Francisco – no surprise to Isabelle. Despite the romantic backdrop, or perhaps because of it, Isabelle hated San Francisco. It reminded her of living there a decade ago, when she met Arnie and they fell in love. Everything was so different now. Seeing the old places they used to go didn't bring back fond memories. They simply reminded her of all the promises he made when they were younger – big ideas he had and plans that never came to fruition.

She missed the hopes and dreams she once held onto. She missed exploring the city together, hiking steep, paved streets for an adrenaline rush, making love in a tiny apartment that permeated the musty scent of summer, and willingly sacrificing friendships to build something with Arnie that she now feared was crumbling around her. How had things changed so much in one short decade? The man, who once made her so happy, had over time come to represent everything she promised herself she would never tolerate.

Isabelle had reservations at the Marriott Marquis on Fourth. She always looked forward to her stays there. She especially enjoyed The View Lounge on the thirty-ninth floor. She never went there with Arnie. It was all hers. The memories of past stays and fascinating strangers were exclusively her memories, without his knowledge or input to retell history differently than she remembered. He couldn't leave the most innocent story alone. One time she was describing a watercolor painting she discovered at an art fair at the Wharf; Arnie corrected her five times as she told Zach about dickering with the artist.

Arnie was quick to correct whatever Isabelle said, and she wondered what drove him to always put her in her place around others. Even when something didn't concern him, he would interrupt the conversation to correct her in front of others. It would especially infuriate her when he would jokingly add, "Tell the truth, Izz. Tell the truth." He thought this was so funny, but she never found it the least bit amusing, especially because he genuinely got at least half the details wrong. She believed it called into question her integrity, even though he said it jokingly and mostly for the reaction it produced. And so when she told stories of people she met at the bar at the top of the Marriott on Fourth, and Arnie jumped in, Isabelle had the distinct pleasure of pointing out that he had never been there and he didn't know what he was talking about. It was her favorite comeback to what she construed to be his unnecessary digs.

Just once Isabelle longed to have her word be the final say – neither interrupted nor corrected by Arnie.

Isabelle was hungry when she checked into the hotel, but she decided she would shower before dinner. Maybe she'd even catch a movie, as that wasn't something she got to enjoy often at home.

When she opened the door to her hotel room, Isabelle was at once both surprised and expectant. *She's back.* She had looked forward to being alone, but she had a visitor. Harriet was there, sitting on the edge of the bed closest to the window watching television.

Isabelle needed to find a way to rectify these visits to make them tolerable if not downright functional. She couldn't help it; she had been looking forward to being alone and Harriet – or some form of her – was encroaching on her space and sanity.

She was feeling snarky. "So we're sharing a room?" she said to the aunt that was – was, she didn't know what she was. A figment of her imagination?

She smiled slightly. *Zach and Arnie would have fun with this.* Isabelle spent a lot of time considering what Zach or Arnie would think of any given thing. It wasn't important why she cared but rather that she did so much.

"I never thought you'd get here," Harriet said. "I'm starving and dying for some great Chinese food."

So this Harriet eats food?

"Well, we're not having Chinese tonight. Too far," Isabelle informed. "Besides, I've been looking forward to eating at the bar upstairs and catching a movie, since I have the time."

"Too far? It's a short taxi ride. Oh, you want to take a trolley?" Harriet questioned.

"I'm not taking you out in public," Isabelle said, partially afraid – and equally hopeful – she wasn't talking to herself.

"I guess some things never change," Harriet said. "I'll wait here and you can bring me back leftovers, maybe?"

Isabelle felt so frustrated she wanted to cry. Somehow she needed to liberate her pent-up emotions. She was losing everything she knew, much of what she loved, and now this.

"This isn't happening. I don't know what this is but whatever it is, it's not happening. Don't follow me," Isabelle insisted as she unzipped her overnight bag, pulled out a small purse, picked up the hotel key card and walked out the door.

She rode the elevator with four strangers and waited for the valet to motion for a cab. She got in alone. She rode alone. Harriet did not follow her tonight. Isabelle sighed in relief. She noticed the taxi driver glancing back at her. When he asked where she wanted to go, she oddly found herself requesting the one place she didn't want to go. China Town.

Why not? Maybe she could finally cross the House of Nanking off her bucket list. Arnie was never game to stand in a line that snaked around the block for dinner. He always insisted on making reservations or going to some dive where he could be immediately seated. But truth be told, Isabelle didn't really want to stand in a line that long either, so she asked to be dropped on Columbus at Brandy Ho's.

As much as she was thrilled Harriet didn't tag along, and as much as she wanted to avoid any realization that she could be losing her mind, which was another legitimate explanation for these visits, Isabelle feared, she didn't want to forego what might be a once-in-a-lifetime opportunity to finally get answers to some of the questions she had wondered for years. And if there was even a chance of getting those answers, she couldn't let the opportunity to hear her aunt out slip by. At the very least, ordering to-go meant eating Chinese take-out in a hotel room alone. It wasn't an option to which she was entirely opposed.

After placing her order in the semi-crowded, highly noisy restaurant, Isabelle stepped outside to call her daughter to check on her day. Grace didn't ask where Isabelle was and Isabelle didn't volunteer the information. She was always available by cell if Grace needed her, and Isabelle didn't need an innocent comment leading to a lecture by Arnie for not providing unnecessary information about her trip. She wasn't really his anymore to check up on.

Isabelle returned to the hotel with dumplings and chicken chow mein. It was more than enough for two. Harriet did not disappoint; she was sitting in exactly the same spot as when Isabelle left, still watching TV. Isabelle was rather amused that even when she was relaxing, Harriet always preferred to be perfectly coiffed in nylons and power suits with over-pronounced shoulder pads.

"I brought your favorite – dumplings." Isabelle opened the white boxes with red Chinese characters to share with her aunt.

"I wanted the chow mein," Harriet said.

"Well, you're in luck. Chicken chow mein it is," Isabelle beamed.

"I always preferred the pork," Harriet noted.

"Of course you did. But it's chicken tonight." Isabelle grinned.

"As long as it's what you like," Harriet said. This conversation was a familiar replica of the kinds of conversations that had driven Isabelle crazy for years. Her aunt was incapable of simply saying thank you, even in this weird space in which she existed now. "I'm just glad I didn't go and embarrass you," Harriet added. This too was a familiar comment Isabelle had grown exhausted of hearing.

Isabelle quickly flipped the conversation. She needed to sort out the circumstances of these visits in her own mind. Was it all her imagination or in her semi-conscious state – *could Harriet actually be in two places at once?*

She watched as Harriet ate, just as normally as if she were really there. *Was she really there?*

Isabelle boldly made the assumption her aunt could potentially be in two places simultaneously, and went with it. "Did you feel anything – before the aneurism?" Isabelle paused. Harriet didn't immediately answer so she continued. "You know that few people even get to the ER in time with a stroke like that. And you're not out of the woods. You may need surgery. They're monitoring you," Isabelle informed her aunt.

Isabelle understood that if Harriet couldn't answer a few key questions about her own experience, she might have to concede that these conversations and chance meetings were in fact a figment of her own imagination taking highly creative liberties. Isabelle much preferred the idea of taking *highly creative liberties* to the alternative that she might be *losing it*, and the consequences of that beyond a vague colloquialism. But before that consideration could thoroughly terrify Isabelle, the way it might have, Harriet responded.

Harriet nonchalantly explained her experience between bites. "It was like a clap of thunder booming; only it was inside my head. The last thing I remember is falling to the floor and struggling to get my phone out of my pocket. I tried to stay conscious but the pain was worse than anything I've ever known," Harriet paused before finishing her thought. "I prayed for help. I wanted to live, and I guess I did because I'm here," Harriet said. Isabelle wasn't really sure she was where she thought she was. "I do want to thank you for getting me out of there," Harriet said.

"There?" Isabelle asked.

"The hospital. The nurses are kind and provide such wonderful care, but I've never been one to sleep for days at a time. And when did you and Zach start to bicker all the time? It's over the top," Harriet said, more as a statement than a question. Isabelle suddenly became defensive. This really wasn't any of her business. She couldn't let it go.

Her cheeks turned a light shade of pink with a splotchy pattern, the way they always did when she was suddenly overcome with intense emotion beyond what she could readily process intellectually. "He used to protect me, but since college he's been picking on me the way you do," Isabelle was all too happy to point out.

"I was always a disappointment to you," Harriet mused.

"Pfft. I felt the same way – that I was the disappointment to you. You picked at everything I did. Nothing was ever good enough. Like last night when you took Arnie's side about bad-mouthing me to Grace. Really? What was that about?" Isabelle asked, between bites.

"Well you can't emasculate a man and expect him to stick around," Harriet advised. And then her tone turned unexpectedly. "You should trust me on that. I probably wasn't always as supportive as Frank wanted, either. He didn't move out but he left in his own way," Harriet said. That was a lot for Isabelle to take in from the woman who had never apologized or admitted fault for anything she had ever done or said. Isabelle decided to silently take a point on that one and let it go.

"It took me fifty years to figure out that men would rather be respected than loved," Harriet told Isabelle.

"So you're an expert on men now?"

"I'm an expert on learning from my mistakes," the motherly aunt explained.

"Hmm. What do you think of the dumplings? Pretty good?" Isabelle asked, changing the subject, smiling and looking for approval.

"Salty. Not my favorite," Harriet said.

"Like that. Why couldn't you just say, 'They're great. Thanks, Isabelle?'"

"You asked what I thought. I thought you wanted to know what I thought. Am I just supposed to tell you they're great if I think they're salty? You didn't make them. It's not like

27

you made them salty. Fine, they're great," Harriet said, completely put out by Isabelle's expectations.

"It's just that sometimes, it's nice to be polite, to be positive, and to be appreciative. Just say thank you and that you appreciate someone going out to get you food, Chinese food, at your request, and bringing it back, to have dinner with you." Isabelle paused and the room went silent aside from the television in the background. "Sometimes a simple thank you will do." Isabelle shrugged.

Isabelle tried to hide her sudden realization that everything that had driven her crazy about Harriet all these years had now become the same exact traits Arnie complained about in her.

Harriet fixed her hair with her hands. "Well, you asked what I thought. I thought you wanted to know. You should have given me a script and told me what you wanted me to say." Harriet was not intentionally sarcastic, despite how she came across. She was as genuinely frustrated by the exchange as Isabelle, perpetuating a pattern that had been in play since about the time Harriet first started dressing in 1980s power suits.

"I want you to treat me the way you have always treated your friends – or Carrie, for that matter – nicely, thoughtfully, and sweetly," Isabelle said.

"You don't have to be jealous of Carrie," Harriet said.

"I'm not jealous of her. I just think you treat her nicely. You don't pick on her the way you do me," Isabelle clarified, and dug at the same time.

"I treat you nicely and my friends nicely. How would you know how I treat my friends? You haven't been around my friends since you were a teenager. You're too busy to spend time with me, let alone with my friends," Harriet argued.

Isabelle stopped. They were getting nowhere. This dumb

conversation could have gone on endlessly, and if it had been their last, Isabelle knew it would mean walking away without any real answers. She wanted answers. She needed answers. And at some point, she needed to find out if this was her mind playing some sort of trick on her or if this was an unexplainable dimension of Harriet that might help her better understand her own life and how she got here.

"Do you know that this is 2015 and that while you're sitting here with me, dressed like it's 1990, by some strange factor that I haven't fully figured out, you're also seventy years old and very sick in a hospital bed in Portland? Do you know that?" Isabelle asked her aunt point blank.

"Of course I know that. I'm not stupid. You talk to me like I'm stupid," Harriet said. "You asked me earlier if I remembered having the stroke. Of course I do. I remember everything. I know what's going on," Harriet said.

Isabelle threw her hands in the air. "Well that makes one of us because I don't know what's going on. It's clearly confusing for me having you in two places at once. And oddly, I believe it's possible. So I'm just trying to figure out if you're a figment of my imagination or if you're here, really here, eating chow mein and complaining – or if this is all me, and I'm putting words in your mouth," Isabelle stumbled through.

"It's strange for me too. I am in both places. I'm here, and I'm there. In fact, there's a nurse taking my blood pressure right now. She's pretty. She looks like your cousin, Ella, Frank's sister's youngest daughter," Harriet described.

"I know who Ella is. Does she have a name tag on? The nurse. Is the nurse wearing a badge?"

"Yes, but I can't read it. It's turned around. She's really happy that I opened my eyes though. It's great to make someone that happy by doing something so common. You'd think I invented the cure for cancer or something," Harriet said.

"Well, that's good. It probably means you're improving. You didn't wake up when we were there last night. You've been on a machine to hyperventilate you and bring down the pressure in your skull ever since your stroke. It's likely you'll need surgery. I'm waiting for Zach to let me know if he's heard anything new," Isabelle said.

Of course Isabelle wanted her aunt to be okay, but before she recovered fully, Isabelle needed answers. The Harriet of today side-stepped Isabelle's questions or said she couldn't remember. Isabelle had so many questions, mostly about her own mom, Harriet's sister, and dad, prior to the car accident that took her parents and changed her life in an instant.

"Harriet, what was your life like growing up, when you and mom were kids?" Isabelle asked.

Harriet finished her food and stood up to throw the wrappers in the trash. When she walked back across the room, she sat down in the hotel desk chair rather than on the side of the bed. "It was different from life today. Of course mom and dad had the farm and everything revolved around that. We had cherries, pears, apples, so from the time dad started disking in the spring, until the last of the red and golden delicious came off in mid October, we basically had school and work at home."

"That sounds harsh," Isabelle said.

Harriet smiled and leaned back into her chair. "It was a great life. I never realized it, I suppose, until it was gone. We did work hard, especially during harvest. We didn't eat out at restaurants or attend social events like when you and Zach were little," Harriet paused to look in the mirror above the desk and move her left eyelid with her finger, as if she had a lone eyelash that needed to come out.

"When Frank and I got married, his work transferred him to Oregon. He moved up in his company quickly, and we adapted to a new way of life. My role supported his career and

I enjoyed playing the hostess and getting involved with new friends and a new life in the city – at least at first. But I never forgot where I came from. I was still a farm girl at heart."

"Did you miss my mom and your parents?" Isabelle asked.

"Of course. Still do," she paused. "Joy was my person." Tears filled her eyes just enough to make them glassy but not so much as to spill over the eyelids immediately. This was a vulnerable side Isabelle had never seen – a side she longed to see, even though she never knew it until now. "When Frank got transferred, we thought it would be for a few years. He let me visit Washington as much as I wanted, but I also wanted to be with him. He was my husband." Harriet paused and tilted her head before continuing, "And he had a bit of a roving eye, to be completely honest." Harriet smirked. Frank had been dead for twenty-one years, and her dismay over that had passed a long time ago. So it truly was something she could snicker about now.

"I wanted your mom to move to Portland. She was going to. I just knew she would love all the exciting things to do – the theatre, the small cafes with artisan bread. The shopping! We had no shopping in Ellensburg. The closest mall was in Yakima and even in its heyday the best thing it had going for it was a Nordstrom. Some of the wives of Frank's coworkers were part of a garden club. I didn't have a green thumb at first, but it was something Joy and I were planning to do together when she moved. She would have loved it," Harriet reminisced.

"So mom was planning to move to Portland?" Isabelle questioned.

"We talked about it. But then she met your dad, and that changed everything. He was a decent man, and he was good for her. He made her happy." Harriet paused and looked away, clearly fighting back tears. Then all at once, as tears popped over her lids and ran down her face, Harriet started to laugh. "Joy had this little yellow house with a garden. Well, it didn't start out a garden. It was pretty much a rock pile with soil mixed in." Harriet wiped her face.

"She'd pick up the rocks and put them in a pile. This whole corner of her yard was basically one big pile of rocks that had come from the garden. Each year, this garden would sink more and more as she pulled out more rocks. She grew everything: tomatoes, cucumbers, eggplant, summer squash, everything. But it was pitiful to look at." Harriet was aglow talking about the sister she still missed and profoundly loved more than three decades later.

"So your dad came along and he was determined to figure out something to do with all those rocks. But he didn't tell your mom. He didn't ask her. He just had his own ideas. He was living with his folks when they met, so when they got married he moved into her house. Took her to Canada for their honeymoon, and when they got back, he had hired some guy to take all those rocks and build a wall around the property. He didn't tell any of us about his plans ahead of time. We were all as surprised as she was." Harriet stopped.

"When your mom saw it the first time, she just said, 'Hmmm.' Nothing else. Just 'hmmm.' You'd think Jack would have told dad or someone. But nope. He just did it. He was like that." Harriet let out a long sigh. "He had some other stuff done to the house while they were away too. He had their bedroom painted green. I always thought that was a weird color for a bedroom. It felt almost secretive at the time, all those changes he was making, but looking back, maybe it wasn't as enigmatic as mom, dad and I assumed. He was probably just trying to create something new for the two of them out of house that had previously been all Joy's," Harriet had a puzzled look on her face.

"What is it?" Isabelle asked, clearly aware there was something her aunt wasn't telling her.

"I don't know. Really, I don't. You know when you sense

something but you can't put your finger on it?"

"Yes," Isabelle immediately offered, nodding, hoping her expressions would prompt her aunt to keep sharing.

"I never really thought about it until now, but there was so much about your dad I never really had an understanding about. And of course I was wrapped up in my own life and so it wasn't like I asked questions or gave it much thought," Harriet said.

"Thought about what?" Isabelle wanted to know. *What was Harriet talking about?*

It was too late. The moment had passed and Harriet had moved on. "Joy wanted a white picket fence, but she never told Jack that. I told her she should have told him, but she said telling him after the fact wouldn't change it. Later, she said she loved his rock wall more than the fence she had planned. I don't think she did. How could she? But that's the story she stood by. It actually wasn't such a terrible idea. What else were they going to do with all those rocks? Could have had them hauled off I guess."

Isabelle, too, had finished eating and cleaned up. She sat at the edge of the bed and crossed her arms. "I remember that wall around the yard. I didn't know all those rocks came from her garden?" Isabelle restated, almost in disbelief.

"There were a lot of rocks in that garden. Your dad may have had some brought in for all I know. He certainly didn't talk to me about it. Then!" Harriet exclaimed and paused for effect, "Jack brought in all this top soil to replace the rocks." Harriet laughed. "Of course nothing grows in just top soil, and Jack didn't know enough to mix compost with it – or ask anyone who would have known. I could have told him that but he didn't ask me." Harriet shook her head.

"The first time I visited her and saw that wall, and the garden where pretty much everything died until dad hauled in some horse manure a year later, I knew she wasn't ever moving to Portland. So I joined the arboretum board as my way of giving back to the community and doing something I knew meant a lot to Joy, and something that always reminded me of her. It was a way we could be close, even if she was miles away." Harriet looked Isabelle squarely in her eyes. "I would have hated Jack if he hadn't loved her so much. But he loved her, and that's really all that mattered," Harriet said.

"What was my dad like?" Isabelle asked.

"He was independent. He did his own thing," Harriet summarized.

"Did mom like that about him?"

"I don't know what she liked. But she never tried to change him," Harriet answered.

"We all start out that way," Isabelle laughed.

Harriet's smile turned downward. "When did you start trying to change Arnie?" Harriet asked.

Isabelle knew Harriet wouldn't let it go, so she just went with it. She let out a big sigh. "When Grace came along I thought we'd both become more responsible. We were in our thirties so it seemed like a no brainer – to me. But Arnie's always chasing the dream. Even today. I grew up and I guess I resented that he didn't." Isabelle was more honest about her feelings toward Arnie in that moment than she had ever been. Admitting the truth seemed like such an enormity, but owning her feelings finally felt right. "Sometimes I think about Masingho – not to look-him-up. More just what if," Isabelle reminisced.

"You were kids!" Harriet exclaimed.

"We were in college and then a couple years after. We weren't any younger than you when you met Frank," Isabelle drew a direct correlation.

"That was a different time," Harriet clarified. "No wonder you struggle with Arnie. You compare him to a fantasy from your youth."

"No," Isabelle scratched her head. "No. Masingho wasn't a fantasy or puppy love. He was brilliant and serious. He made me feel safe. He understood business – and me. He thought I was amazing." Isabelle clarified. Even she was taken aback by how strongly she still felt almost two decades later. Harriet didn't interject. Isabelle even paused to give Harriet the chance to jump in, but her aunt remained mum.

"Arnie was amazing too. He was just amazing in a different way. Arnie was fun. He is fun. He can be fun, anyway. When there are no consequences. When there are no bills and no honey-do lists. Arnie was exactly what I needed when I met him. He was my escape from a great, deep, penetrating love." Isabelle was starkly aware of how this sounded, and she didn't mean it to come out this way.

"Arnie is a great dad. If I hadn't gotten pregnant, and I hadn't married Arnie, I might be alone and without Grace or anyone today," Isabelle popped air into one cheek and then let it slide out her lips making a funny sound. "Arnie was a great boyfriend. We probably should have been friends with benefits but not actually gotten married." Isabelle couldn't believe she just said this to her aunt. It wasn't something Harriet wanted to hear either. "I didn't set out to change him. But as I said, I grew up and I thought he would too."

Silence fell over the room for nearly a minute before Harriet picked the conversation up where she left off. "Joy got pregnant on their honeymoon or soon after. Zach was here ten months later, almost to the day. Mom kept counting back the weeks, for years. Now I guess it doesn't matter. Joy insisted he was conceived on the honeymoon."

Isabelle fluttered her eyes and sighed. "Why would that matter?" *Did Harriet not just hear her say that she was pregnant when she and Arnie got married?*

"Your generation is so liberal today. You just go with what you feel. We didn't do that back then," Harriet explained.

"They loved each other, clearly, so why did it matter?" Isabelle asked a question but intended it more as a statement. "Were you there when Zach or I was born?"

"Mom and I were both there for Zach's birth and for yours two years later. You were both perfect babies. Beautiful. Healthy. You cried a lot. You were very colicky," Harriet pointed out.

"I tried to be as colicky as possible," Isabelle sarcastically added. Harriet tilted her head and gave Isabelle a confused look as if she didn't realize for a moment she was joking.

"Some kids just are," Harriet said. "So what are you going to do about Arnie? Certainly you don't want to be a single parent. You must have thought about that."

I think about that every freaking day.

As close as Isabelle and Harriet were one minute, the smallest comments put the two women at odds. The combination was a modern day tinder box, because despite their glaring and obvious differences, they shared similarities that neither of them cared to admit.

"It's late, Harriet, and I need to be at the conference at seven-thirty tomorrow morning. I need to go to bed." She reached for the remote and turned the television off. She wasn't sure what would happen next. Harriet was a night owl. Isabelle liked to think of herself as more practical in terms of good sleeping patterns. But the truth was that they both let time slip away from them.

"You can sleep here or go back to the hospital. Your choice," Isabelle said as she headed to the bathroom. Isabelle washed her face, crawled in bed and turned out the light.

◆ ◆ ◆

Normally, when Isabelle arrived back from a trip, she didn't return to the office. But her flight arrived a little after noon, and since Grace still had a couple of hours of school left and there was no way for Isabelle to predict how Harriet's condition might change, she decided to drive to her office in downtown Portland.

When she drove into the underground parking beneath her building, she immediately found a parking spot. *Sweet!* Walking to the elevator, an older lady with gray hair and an oversized coat approached her. "Excuse me, ma'am. Do you have any change you can spare?" the lady asked.

Isabelle was not a fan of drifters and panhandlers, but instead of pretending like she didn't hear her ask for help, she stopped. She took a deep breath, turned around and looked the woman directly in her eyes. The woman wasn't just older – she was much older. She looked to be close to Harriet's age. *She must have had a hard life to be homeless at this age.* "Let me see what I have," Isabelle said, as she opened her wallet. She had more cash than usual, having just returned from a trip. She had two twenties, three tens, two fives and a short stack of ones.

Isabelle started to reach for a dollar. *What if you needed help? What if you didn't have money for your next meal? Where would you turn? Wouldn't you hope some kind person would help you out without making you feel like their charity deed of the day?* Isabelle's hand slid across a paper bill. She looked up and pressed her lips together as the woman's eyes grew larger and took on that sense of embracing hopefulness. Isabelle took a deep breath and smiled as she handed the woman a folded bill.

The woman looked down at the bill, clearly in shock. "Did you mean to hand me a twenty?" the woman asked, clearly perplexed.

"Yes!" Isabelle said, definitively. "Enjoy a nice lunch somewhere," Isabelle said, as she waved, lifted her heels and turned on the balls of her feet and resumed walking toward the elevator in one smooth, quick motion.

"Your generosity will be returned to you someday," the woman called out. Isabelle could think of many areas of her life that she'd like to summons a genie in a bottle to correct, but aside from a quick chuckle, she didn't read much into the woman's sincere appreciation.

CHAPTER 3

Isabelle arrived at room ICU-12 with an arrangement of artificial flowers. She hoped Harriet would be alert, or at least awake, and able to enjoy them. Isabelle wasn't a fan of what she called fake flowers, but she had to pick which ICU rules to follow and which to bend. When she arrived, her aunt appeared to be in the same vegetative state as when she left. She was disappointed but didn't let it affect her spirits. She felt strangely good about their visit in San Francisco.

Isabelle sat, legs crossed, in the oversized leather hospital recliner beside her aunt's bed and pulled out her smart phone to respond to a few emails. Just as she started typing, a nurse, who just as Harriet described, had an uncanny resemblance to her cousin, peeked in to check on the patient. And just like in Harriet's description, her name badge was turned around. *It was probably a coincidence.* Clearly her aunt had not been alert enough to make this connection.

Arnie called to let Isabelle know he was bringing Grace up to the second floor. Kids technically weren't allowed in the ICU but the nurses had kindly overlooked this rule, and Isabelle made every attempt to be discreet hoping they would continue to look the other way. Isabelle grabbed her bags and stepped outside the ICU into the family waiting area.

When she heard the patter of running feet, Isabelle instantly recognized the cadence of the approaching skip. Seconds later, Grace showed up. "Daddy and I had ice cream after school today and I got two scoops," Grace informed her mother before Arnie even arrived. Normally, Isabelle would scold Arnie for giving her so much sugar and ruining the child's appetite for dinner. But today, Isabelle paused and nonchalantly slid the orange she brought for Grace back into her jacket pocket right as Arnie walked through the door. They smiled weakly at each other. *Relax, Isabelle. Don't make this a bigger deal than it is.* Isabelle went to great lengths to appear calmer than she felt.

Isabelle was sitting down when Grace jumped into her lap and wrapped her arms around her mom. Arnie hadn't talked to Isabelle about the ice cream, and she felt he should have known she wouldn't approve. But it was done now. So this time, she skipped the lecture altogether, both to Grace and Arnie, and simply inquired about which flavors the child chose. Her eyes opened wide when Grace told her, "It was so yummy."

Maybe Harriet had a point. Maybe she had been unnecessarily hard on Arnie. Maybe, she thought, nagging him the last several years hadn't actually helped him improve, and may have in fact chipped away at their relationship. Isabelle never would have admitted this aloud, but the thought did cross her mind.

Zach arrived a few minutes later, alone, without his willowy girlfriend with the unpleasant demeanor. *What? No whatever-her-name-is didn't follow you?* Zach greeted Arnie as if Isabelle was invisible. The men talked about an upcoming game they both seemed quite enthusiastic about, while Grace sat on Isabelle's lap and told her about every detail of her day at school. Isabelle loved the raw excitement with which Grace always shared her activities. Being the mother of a child who found the whole world and everything in it so amazing filled Isabelle with a sense of wonder and joy. Grace brought magic to Isabelle's world. Isabelle wanted to focus completely on what her little girl was saying, but she kept one ear on the conversation across the room by the vending machine, where Arnie and Zach were laughing and joking. Isabelle remembered when Arnie used to bring magic to her world, when he made everything seem new and possible. But those days were behind them now.

These days, the mere sight of Arnie made Isabelle feel miserable and depressed. She desperately wanted to see him differently – to see him the way she once had. It was as if he had intentionally taken everything that she hoped for and once believed was possible and pushed it off a cliff for it to break in a hundred pieces below.

She had her reasons. Somewhere along the line he stopped investing in a future for the three of them and shifted his attention to hobbies without dividends and fantasy football teams that consumed his time and money. She once thought to herself that if there was one thing she would change about Arnie, it would be how obsessed he was with every sport and every game that entered his peripheral view. But then there were so many other things that drove her just as crazy, so she consciously opted to tune out the men and focus exclusively on her precious daughter in her lap. Acutely aware of how quickly time would pass, she tried to savor every story and moment with the child.

"How was your trip?" Zach interrupted the story about butterflies Grace was telling.

"Your trip? You were gone?" Arnie asked.

"I had a quick conference in San Francisco. It was good. Flight was bumpy but the trip was good," Isabelle shared. Purposefully returning her gaze to Grace, she quickly shifted her focus. "Were there yellow butterflies too?"

Arnie didn't want the subject changed. "You went to San Francisco and didn't tell me?" Arnie questioned his estranged wife.

"It was a quick business trip. You had Grace. I was there less than 24 hours." Isabelle's tone defended her lack of sharing. She had actually wanted to share with Arnie that she was going, but she intentionally held back knowing their relationship was changing and she needed to change in response to that. He was no longer her person. She needed to stop clearing her life with him. He certainly never cleared his with her. Still, while she knew Zach was probably stirring the pot, she was glad he did in this instance. She wanted Arnie to know she was capable of the independence he had often said he wished she'd embrace when she challenged him on the amount of time he devoted to pursuing his own ambitions.

"Did you go," Arnie paused, "anywhere?" He let the question hang. He wanted to ask if she went to any of their favorite places, but he too was editing, assuming she didn't want to share anything with him, or she would have told him about her trip. Isabelle loved watching him squirm because when he did, he looked the way she felt every time they disagreed – restless and unsettled.

As Isabelle replayed the crumbling of their marriage in her mind, there were hundreds of little moments when either of them could have thrown the gears into neutral. This moment would join her closet of regrets unless Arnie took the initiative to turn the conversation around. He didn't.

"Let's see. Did I go anywhere? Well, I had a conference. I went to the conference, Arnie, and I went out to eat and did some shopping. I don't know what you're implying," she said. Isabelle knew exactly what she was implying and what it was doing to him.

In some ways, she felt as if she were giving karma a nudge for how he had made her feel over the years. Isabelle's tone turned lighter as she spoke to Grace. "Do you want to see what I got you?" Her eyes genuinely twinkled when she turned to her child. For seconds Arnie held onto that look. He knew that look of excitement in Isabelle's eyes, excitement that was conspicuously not directed at him.

"What did you get me?" Grace wiggled and squealed. Isabelle pulled out a pastel-colored slicker. It was printed in a pink- and yellow-striped pattern with Minnie Mouse in a hot pink dress and Disney heels just below the left shoulder. Grace loved Minnie Mouse and all things Disney, as did Isabelle.

"Here, try it on," Isabelle prodded. The raincoat fit perfectly and Grace loved it. She twirled around the waiting room in circles like a ballerina before returning to her mother's lap. Isabelle hoped Zach would retract his mother of the year award comment from a few days back, but he didn't. She didn't buy the raincoat to impress her brother, after all. She wanted to make her little girl smile, and that she accomplished.

"Well I guess I'll see you Saturday when I pick up Grace," Arnie said as he walked back toward the elevator.

Arnie and Isabelle had developed a habit of walking out on each other every time the conversation got tense. They bickered, but they didn't fight with each other or for each other, and as such, far too much went unsaid. Years of crunchy, unexpressed emotions had ultimately created two people who didn't talk and each resented the other one for it. At various times, each had suggested counseling, but even then their timing was off. He made efforts when she blew him off and she made efforts when he couldn't make time. About all they had holding them together was the child they both loved. Grace jumped down from her mom's lap and went running down the hall after Arnie to hug her dad goodbye.

Back in the waiting room, Isabelle was left with the other man in her life she didn't understand well and with whom she also struggled to communicate. *Why?* She wondered if it was her – if she was the common denominator. But she quickly dismissed that thought.

"How is Harriet doing?" Zach asked. He didn't look up at Isabelle as he asked. He was typing something on his phone, which gave Isabelle the distinct impression he was making conversation but didn't really care.

"Same," Isabelle said, hoping her one-word answer would get his attention or prompt him to ask if everything was okay. It didn't.

"I suppose we should start thinking about a service," Zach nonchalantly stated. "Do you have a list of people we need to inform when she passes?" he asked. Harriet had been sick in the past and always recovered. Isabelle hadn't even considered that their aunt wouldn't rally once again.

"The doctors haven't given up. Let's not pull the sheet over her head yet," Isabelle snapped at her brother.

"Izz! I'm just saying we ought to prepare ourselves that she may not get better. I know it scares you to think like that but we have to come to terms. And it might be sooner than we're ready for," Zach reasoned. "All I'm saying is we may need to start working on all that funeral stuff, so it's, you know, ready in case." Zach stated this plan as if it was inevitable, which tore at Isabelle more than he understood or intended. Technically, Isabelle knew it was inevitable. But if Harriet held the key to learning more about their mother, Isabelle didn't want to cut short even a minute of her life.

Isabelle didn't mind having their aunt in the hospital so long as she had access to the younger version in her private world, the one with the stories and the answers to Isabelle's questions, hopes and dreams.

"It makes sense to have you write the eulogy," Zach casually said as if he was suggesting she pick up oranges for brunch.

"Why me? Why not you? You're her favorite." Isabelle was resentful that he assumed she would take care of all the details without even asking what she wanted to do. Isabelle longed to feel cared for as she once had by Masingho. First, she had to be the responsible parent who saw to it that the bills were paid and the appliances were maintained at home, and now she had to take responsibility for her aunt too. *Why can't anyone step up and help shoulder the load for me?* "Why do I have to write her eulogy?" Isabelle's tone with Zach was sharper than she intended.

Isabelle hadn't thought of Masingho in years, until his name came up with Harriet. *Why is he suddenly permeating my thoughts?*

"I just assumed you would." Zach said.

Ugg. Why do I have to do everything?

Isabelle wished it was easier to be happy, that there was a pill she could take or a patch perhaps that would make her feel cheerful and carefree again – or at least something to numb the constant disappointment that had become her life. She disliked herself being so petulant. It didn't match the image she held of herself, but it was this unsavory side that increasingly came out, more often than not these days.

What a relief it was for her to have Grace, the one person who didn't make her feel angry and impatient. Grace represented the person Isabelle wanted to be, the person she worked to be, even if that brighter side of her was buried. Grace was joyful, nonchalant, and a natural believer in all things magical. Isabelle was like that as a child too – before the accident.

She didn't like dividing her memories like that, down a line in the sand before the accident and after, but it was her reality. It was the defining moment of her life that whether she liked it or not made everything change from happy and promising to unacceptable and boarder-line surly. That was with the exception of the early days with Arnie. He brought back those feelings of joy and a genuine sense of wonder for the first few years of their relationship, when he worked so hard to win her over – and to which, after some initial resistance, she enjoyed every moment of giving in.

"Look, I'm not trying to go all master of the obvious on you, but sometimes you do sort of have the disposition of a wet cat on a cloudy day. Don't get mad," Zach said.

"How is that master of the obvious? Is that supposed to inspire me to do what you want?"

"Life is hard but it's more fun to be around happy people." Isabelle so badly wanted to turn to him and say it – *now that's master of the obvious* – but she didn't. She didn't have to. It was written on her face. When Zach looked over at her, with what he called her angry-bird smirk on her face, he started laughing. Hysterically. And oddly enough, then so did she. *Stupid brother.* She hated that she knew he was right.

Isabelle stood up and walked over to the door, looking for Grace. When she peeked her head around the corner, she saw the child hugging Arnie at the elevator. Isabelle's heart sank. She knew Grace wanted their little family together, but Arnie too had changed. Instead of growing together they had each changed in ways that intensified their differences. He was not the man she married, and she felt increasingly less like herself. Harriet's constant barrage of corrections, intended to help her niece, had long ago penetrated Isabelle's ridiculously thin skin to the point that today even she couldn't differentiate between what inside of her was worth saving or changing anymore. Losing Arnie felt like the final stage of losing everything she once loved about herself.

She paused at the doorway before turning back to Zach and agreeing to start thinking about writing Harriet's eulogy. How was she supposed to write something meaningful and supportive of the woman she deeply loved but who had spent decades disparaging everything she had ever done, said or thought? It wasn't something she could think about now. It would have to wait for another day.

Zach stood up and walked over to his sister to give her a half hug, arm around her shoulder. "I'm going to check on Harriet," he said. "I'll talk to you later."

"Okay," Isabelle said as she picked up her own coat, purse, bag and Grace's purse, and lumbered down the hall toward Arnie and Grace, arriving just as the elevator door closed with Arnie inside. At the elevator she handed Grace her little girl's purse.

A part of her wanted to run back and tell her aunt to hold on – that she needed more time. But Grace was getting squirmy and Isabelle knew she probably needed to get home and start on homework.

When the elevator doors opened on the main level, a nurse Isabelle didn't recognize looked at her directly, smiled and exclaimed with excitement, "It's you. I know you."

Who is this? Should I know this person? Isabelle smiled and blurted out, "I should know your name, but I don't." It was the first honest admission of weakness Isabelle had made in a long time.

"Sally Jo. You helped my daughter pick out our kitten at the humane society," the nurse said.

It had been months since Isabelle had taken Grace to volunteer at the local animal shelter. It was something she loved but hadn't made time for in her hectic schedule.

"She's getting so big," Sally Jo said. "Her name is Shadow. Let me show you a picture of her," the nurse said as she grabbed her phone out of her scrubs pocket without hesitation. Isabelle's guard came down as she waited with anticipation to see the stranger's cat. *Why don't I remember this lady?* Isabelle searched her own mind for some reference.

Isabelle looked at the cute black cat in the photo and glanced down as Sally Jo moved the phone so that Grace could also see the pictures of her cat. For a moment Isabelle felt like

47

she remembered this black kitten with white paws.

"Shadow has been a godsend. She follows Janie every-where. Thank you," Sally Jo's kind eyes were sincere. Suddenly, Isabelle remembered those eyes, and her little girl with curly black hair. *Yes, of course, I remember.* Isabelle smiled, genuinely pleased with herself for remembering the lady and her daughter. Then she intentionally stopped smiling.

"You lost your mom," Isabelle recalled. "She took care of Janie while you worked and you were looking for a new family member so your daughter wouldn't be so sad about losing her grandma." Isabelle wanted to jump up and down. Lately, she had been forgetting everything, living in a mental slump. But Sally Jo helped her snap out of it. *Make this about her, Isabelle.* "How are you doing?" Isabelle asked.

"It's hard," Sally Jo's eyes filled with tears. Isabelle nod-ded. She understood. Suddenly, Sally Jo looked like she remem-bered she needed to be somewhere else. "I need to get back to the floor. But thank you. Thank you for helping us. Shadow has a great forever home, and you brought joy back to our lives," Sally Jo said as she stepped into the elevator. *I did something good that actually made a difference to someone.* Isabelle exhaled. She was at the same time stunned and excited by the brief but powerful interaction.

When the door closed, Grace took her mom's hand. "When are we going to volunteer at the animal shelter again?"

"Soon. We need to make time to do that," Isabelle said.

Isabelle was hanging up the phone from a call with a client, when one of her co-workers, Tina, dropped by to compliment her on her hair. Not being someone who fraternized much with the women in her office, this gesture caught her off guard. "Thank you," Isabelle said, almost dismissively, immediately looking back at her computer monitor.

"Oh, uh, do you have a brother?" Tina asked, keeping the conversation going past what Isabelle would have preferred.

"Yes," Isabelle said smiling. *You can go away now.*

"I met him. Arnie, right? He goes to my gym," Tina said. Now she had Isabelle's attention.

"Arnie is my husband," Isabelle said, not offering information about their estrangement.

"Your husband? Maybe there's another Arnie," Tina said, making a weird face. "He kissed me after we had drinks last week. I'm sure it's someone else with the same name," she suggested, followed by a duplicitous grin.

Don't take the bait. "What do you mean he kissed you?" Isabelle asked, knowing it wasn't her business, and wishing she hadn't asked. But the words were already out.

"Well, we ended up on side-by-side cardio machines and just started talking – you know how that is. Next thing I knew he had my number and wanted to go out afterward. So we did – and one thing led to another. Gosh, I feel bad now," Tina said.

I had to take the damn bait. It wasn't enough for Arnie to start dating. He had to pick someone I have to see every day. Jack ass.

Isabelle tried to conceal her emotions.

"Well, we're separated," Isabelle reluctantly confessed. It pained her to share a single drop of her personal information at work. It was bad enough that Salvador, her boss, needed to know about Harriet.

"I'm so sorry," Tina walked into Isabelle's office from just standing in the doorway, and sat down without being invited. "I feel just terrible." She didn't look sorry.

"Well, it's hard. We have a daughter and eight years of marriage. Ten years together," Isabelle said. Isabelle glanced up at their family photo on the cherry wood cabinet across the room. She did not want to have this conversation with anyone, let alone a virtual stranger at work.

Tina would not give up. "So do you think you will work things out? I would never want to be a home wrecker. You just say the word and I'll back off," Tina said. It was hard for Isabelle to be upset with someone who appeared to be an innocent party in all of this, despite her incongruent body language.

"Look, I really need to finish this report by four-thirty. I appreciate your concern but I don't really know you and I'm not terribly comfortable with this conversation," Isabelle confided.

Tina looked taken back, as she slowly placed her palm on her chest and inhaled in an exaggerated manner. "Oh I'm so sorry. If I would have had any idea, I never would have, gosh, I just feel so bad," she said, starting several thoughts without finishing the last.

"It's not your problem. It's fine. Thank you. I'm sorry but I really need to get back to this," Isabelle said, turning back to her monitor. She was seething at Arnie by this time.

When Tina left her office, Isabelle stood up and walked over to shut the door. While up, she picked up their family picture, opened a drawer, and placed it upside down in the drawer before pushing it closed.

Why would he want to move back in if he was seeing someone new? Wouldn't he at least mention that we should be seeing other people so I could prepare myself for this?

Isabelle's phone buzzed. It was a daily affirmation from a site she had subscribed to receiving messages. *I receive love and support because I deserve it.* Isabelle rolled her eyes, shook her head and moved her finger to delete the message. But just before she deleted it, she reconsidered. She read it again. This time aloud. *I receive love and support because I deserve it.*

Then she deleted it.

Isabelle took a deep breath and tuned everything out except her report. Her schedule left no room for daydreaming if she expected to get everything done and keep everything going. She needed to focus – now.

◆ ◆ ◆

That evening, in making dinner, Isabelle dished up the chicken breast and frosted cauliflower, baked with a mustard spread and shredded reduced-fat cheese melted over the top. It was one of Grace's favorites, and gave Isabelle some sense that she was getting solid nutrients along with whatever junk food Arnie was feeding her. Grace used to love salads and picking out a creative and colorful palate of vegetables, before Arnie left. Now she asked for drive-through food and frozen chicken nuggets.

Isabelle admitted to herself that she had grown increasingly strict in the foods she brought into the house after Grace started eating grown-up food with them. It was intended to set a good example, but like with other things, Isabelle's meal planning bordered on extreme. She knew Arnie was more than happy to eat frozen pizza rolls heated in the microwave. It was because she loved him that she wanted to change him – for the better – for his own sake. Now it didn't matter. Her decisions had to be in the best interest of Grace.

"What do you think dad is having for dinner?" Grace asked her mom.

"I don't know," Isabelle said, debating how to take this conversation. Should she ignore her daughter's obvious desire to keep Arnie in the house, at dinner, in their lives, or should she address the elephant in the room? "Grace, Dad will always love you and we will always work together to do what is best for you. But honey, barring a miracle, he's not moving back in. He might have dinner with us sometimes, but probably more often he will have dinner somewhere else."

"I believe in miracles," Grace said, her soulful eyes searching for a positive reaction. "I wish he were here. Do you wish he was here?"

Isabelle's heart sank. She thought for a moment before responding. "Honey, I know it's getting dark, but take a look at that tree in the yard over by the mailbox. See how it has one trunk and a little ways up that one trunk gets a little smaller and splits into two big branches with lots of little branches coming off of it?"

After staring intently at the tree, majestic in the moonlight, with just a bit of dusk sunlight hanging on the horizon, the little girl nodded yes. "Both big, strong branches are part of the same tree, but you see the point where they each go in their own direction. It makes the tree pretty and it's better for each of the branches to have room to develop. Daddy and I need our own room to branch and grow. We're like that tree, still connected by the trunk, still connected by you – but each with our own space."

Grace stared across the yard and then turned her attention to the other trees in the yard. Pointing at a tall red maple she said, "That tree has one trunk and lots of tiny branches and it has the most beautiful red leaves. Its branches don't need space. It makes pretty leaves and only has one trunk."

Why did she have to be so smart? Isabelle mused silently, ultimately knowing her critical thinking skills were a very good thing, although somewhat inconvenient in this exact moment.

"Yes, indeed, so you see, to have a pretty yard, we need all kinds of trees," Isabelle said. "Trees with branches that split apart and trees where they don't. One isn't better or worse.

What matters is that all the trees are healthy, watered, fertilized and cared for."

Grace seemed at the same time both accepting of and disillusioned by her mom's analogy. It was clear, Grace would be giving this conversation more thought. But in the meantime, she changed the subject, like she had witnessed her parents do hundreds of times when one of them was avoiding a fight, "I have a history quiz tomorrow. Will you help me study for it?"

"Of course I will," Isabelle agreed. Isabelle knew instinctively that she should have circled back and vetted Grace's questions. A part of her wanted desperately to do this for the sake of her daughter's development – and perhaps to correct the role Harriet had played in her own development decades before. But the sacrifice to herself was simply too great and she too quickly seized the opportunity Grace presented to change the subject to the impending history exam.

It was just easier.

After dinner was finished, and the dishes were rinsed and set in the dishwasher, Grace pulled her backpack on wheels out to the dining room table and reached for her textbook, bookmarked to the chapter she needed to know for the quiz.

"I think the Oregon Trail should have been called the Independence Trail," Grace shared, in what seemed like a completely out-of-context observation.

"What's that?" Isabelle inquired.

"The Oregon Trail. With Lewis and Clark," Grace reminded her mom of third grade history.

"Because," Isabelle paused before adding, "They found their independence on a long, difficult road?" Isabelle questioned.

"Uh, no. Because it started in Independence, Missouri and Oregon didn't even exist as a state at the time." Grace seemed perplexed that her mom didn't readily seem to know this. Grace's wide eyes were looking for some sort of connection to confirm this wasn't a completely unfamiliar topic to her mom.

"Well, it was a territory, wasn't it?" Isabelle asked. *I thought it started in St. Louis, at the arch.* Isabelle didn't remember enough to actually add anything to the discussion. *This would be a good opportunity to practice my listening skills.* "Why don't you tell me about it?"

"Families walked thousands of miles and rode in covered wagons that were highly primitive. But they wanted to see the Pacific Ocean so they packed everything up and became pioneers."

"Highly primitive. Well, that sounds like a fun adventure," Isabelle prompted.

"A lot of them got sick and died. It doesn't sound that fun," Grace stated the obvious.

"When you put it like that..." Isabelle intentionally didn't finish her sentence. She wanted to see how her daughter was processing this lesson.

"But there were explorers who drew maps. I could have been an explorer. Or joined the Pony Express and delivered mail and messages. That might have been fun."

"You can be anything you set your mind to," Isabelle said.

"That's not totally logical, but I appreciate the sentiment," Grace said.

Isabelle was overcome with how much Grace reminded her of Arnie sometimes. *That's exactly the kind of thing he would say.* Isabelle wanted to argue with Grace, to convince her otherwise. Isabelle did not want to support this limiting way of thinking.

"I'm only eight. What if I'm short? Then I couldn't be a supermodel," Grace reasoned.

Isabelle had to give her that one. Isabelle shrugged. "I guess you got me there." *Was it so wrong of her to want her daughter to believe that anything she dreamed of was possible? It was better than her imagining that she had to fit into someone else's vision or stereotype of who she might grow up to be.*

Isabelle didn't want to rush her daughter through her homework. And at the same time, Isabelle hoped that if Grace went to bed, Harriet might be more inclined to visit. And she very much wanted to connect with her. Isabelle was becoming increasingly excited about her developing relationship with this alternate version of her aunt. It began to preoccupy her thoughts even when she knew it was important to stay in the moment. If there was anything she was recognizing from her time with Harriet, it was how short life was when you want to hang onto it. And as much as she wanted answers from her past, answers about her own mom, those answers wouldn't mean anything if the search for them cost her a single moment in the present with her own daughter, who in every way had become her world.

And so despite her hope to meet up with her past, she stayed in the moment with her daughter, engaged first in her lessons, and then in helping her get ready for bed. As the two generations sat on the side of the pink ruffled bed, Grace surprised her mom with some unusual questions, "Are you thinking about Yia Yia? Do you miss her?" That's exactly who Isabelle was thinking about, although in a much different way than she believed Grace could have imagined.

Isabelle stroked her daughter's hair. "Yes, honey, I miss her. I was thinking about her. You are such a smart little girl," Isabelle hugged the eight-year-old. And when she did, the most amazing thing happened. Isabelle felt as if someone was hugging her, only not as the mom. Isabelle felt like her eight-year-old self was somehow being hugged. And for the first time since she was Grace's age, she felt a deep comfort she had not experienced since her own parents died. She unexpectedly felt utterly relaxed, in a way her adolescent and adult selves never had. It took her daughter holding her on the side of the bed that night to reach the sad and closed off part of her heart that had been beating ever so shallow inside her body for more than three decades.

Isabelle inhaled deeply as if smelling one of the roses from her mother's garden, and exhaled like she was blowing out the candles on the last birthday cake her mom had ever baked. It was an exercise a therapist had suggested years ago, but that resonated with Isabelle. Acknowledging the intense calm the breathing exercises brought about, she repeated the pattern a few more times. Suddenly, in the arms of her daughter, Isabelle felt completely safe – safer than she ever had with Harriet and Frank, Zach or even Arnie. Safer even than with Masingho.

For the first time in Isabelle's entire life, she actually felt whole.

When her little girl suggested a prayer for Yia Yia, Isabelle went along with her request knowing it was probably a habit her dad had started. There was a time Isabelle prayed quite a lot, but somehow in the hustle and disappointment of life, it was as if she didn't know what to say anymore and she wasn't even completely sure anymore her prayers were heard. The two kneeled, and Isabelle listened to the faith of a child pour out to God, or whoever was listening.

"Dear God, please help me get an A on my history quiz tomorrow. And be with mommy as she is scared that Yia Yia is going to die. Please don't let her die until she is over a hundred, or something very very old. Please help mommy not to be so sad because if mommy is sad, we will never get the puppy I want. A puppy would be fun and I would feed her. Please help daddy come home."

Isabelle cringed.

Grace continued without noticing. "Bless us and keep us safe while we sleep. Amen."

Isabelle remained kneeling for a bit, thinking. Now she knew what was on her daughter's mind. She had to admire her daughter's inclination toward the power of positive thinking.

"Will you snuggle with me?" Grace asked her mom, after she was all tucked in.

"Of course." She slid into the left side of the bed. Isabelle cradled the child against her, and soon Grace was fast asleep. Isabelle could have gotten up. She even thought about it for a moment. But she knew she was exactly where she needed to be, and so she stayed until she got up and changed for bed herself.

CHAPTER 4

When Isabelle walked into the gym to spend her lunch hour on the elliptical machine, she cringed when she saw Harriet already on the machine next to the only empty one. And she cringed even more when she waved and motioned her over. "I saved a machine for you," Harriet called out to her.

While Isabelle wanted nothing more than to spend time alone with Harriet, she hated the idea of talking to someone in public who she hadn't determined was real. It wasn't as if she could ask a stranger if they could see her aunt. What if they couldn't? Isabelle visited the gym regularly and wasn't sure she could joke about their answer – whichever way it went. So she went with it. Smiling and nodding, but not waving across the room.

Just act natural.

To further complicate Isabelle's understanding of the situation, how was it that in the middle of a crowded gym, only the machine next to Harriet remained open? Unless the possibility existed that Harriet was actually there and others could see her?

Isabelle realized this was the first time Harriet had visited her not dressed like a 1980s PTA mom. Today, Harriet was wearing a velour jogging suit, top and bottom matching of course, and tennis shoes that looked to be new. *Ha! Even Harriet is capable of change!* Just in case her fears were true, Isabelle put a Bluetooth in her ear at the locker where she shoved her belongings before heading to the cardio zone.

Isabelle climbed onto the machine, set a bottle of water into the plastic cup holder, and nodded hello to the people on both sides of her, a stranger and of course Harriet. "How's your day going?" Harriet asked.

Oh not yet. She really wished her aunt would at least let her get settled and plug her personal information into the machine before she launched a public conversation, even a non-threatening one. Harriet asked again.

Isabelle reached over and appeared to answer a call on her phone, in case anyone was paying attention – which they were not. Like most people in Isabelle's self-conscious state, she was far more important in her own mind than to the strangers in the world around her. Isabelle was oblivious to how uninvolved strangers were to her whereabouts. "Good, how are you?"

"You've been wanting to talk. You're busy, so I thought I'd show up here. Save you some time. I will need for you to give me a ride home afterward, though," Harriet said.

Home? Like home, home, or the hospital?

"Well, I'm at the gym, I'm not sure this is a good time. I don't want to disrupt the other members. Can we catch up later?" Isabelle asked into her microphone earpiece.

"We need to talk now. I'm heading into surgery," Harriet shared. "They are prepping me now."

Isabelle's eyes narrowed. "Oh, I had no idea. Doctors said it was a possibility, but I hadn't heard that anything was scheduled. What does this mean for the project?" Isabelle felt conflicted. She wondered if she should really be at the gym right now, instead of holding what seemed to be an important conversation with or about Harriet. Isabelle could sense an urgency building, as if time was running out. She could sense deep inside that her life was about to change forever, and she felt completely unable to change, fix or alter it.

No more waiting. But what should I do?

Harriet was there now, at the gym. She wouldn't be back. So many questions ran through her mind. Should she just stay for twenty more minutes and then go straight to the hospital? Should she leave now? God knew her heart rate was elevated beyond what any workout would provide. She almost struggled to catch deep breaths. *Not another stupid anxiety attack now.* She had to make a decision soon. Seconds felt like minutes and minutes like hours. Time was slipping through her fingers at a rate that made her painfully aware of everything she had at risk.

A woman near her was reading the television captions aloud and spontaneously sharing her commentary about the events of the day. Normally this would bother Isabelle, but today it was barely a distraction. The stranger on the machine to her left leaned over to Isabelle and said, "Most people aren't out to annoy us. They were just raised differently," with a quick smile and then an even quicker turn of her head to face back forward. In her paranoid state, Isabelle took these words personally for a few seconds, wondering what she meant by this. Then just as suddenly, she dismissed her and let it go.

Isabelle had to go. She jumped off the machine and ran over to the station with paper towels and wipes. Even in a hurry, Isabelle would not leave a machine messy for the next person. She rushed to the locker and grabbed her belongings, clicking the button to unlock her car the second she passed through the front door. Harriet was right behind her.

In the car, Isabelle felt free to talk. "So tell me what is going on?" she almost demanded.

"They wheeled my bed somewhere in a hurry after the

nursing supervisor told some other nurses they needed to get me to pre-op stat." She looked out the window and her voice went grave. "That's it. That's the last thing I heard." If there was ever a time Isabelle wished Harriet could have expanded on a situation, it was now, but she had nothing more to add.

This is it.

"Harriet," Isabelle said before pausing, "thank you. For all you and Frank did for Zach and me."

Harriet brought her hand up to her face. "Well, you know I did what anyone would do, both for you and for Joy. It wasn't…" Harriet was cut off by her niece.

"No, don't ruin this moment with a big long soliloquy," Isabelle said. "Just say, 'Honey, I love you. You're welcome. I wouldn't have changed a thing.'"

Now Harriet crossed her arms. "You want me to say what you want, not what I want." Harriet was agitated.

"Yes, in this case, let's leave it good. Let's leave it positive." Isabelle reached her right hand over and held the elderly hands of her aunt. "If this is the end, I want to miss you. I will miss you. I love you and I will always love you," Isabelle said, tears in her eyes. "I love you so much. But I don't want to fight with you or be exasperated by a long over-telling of nothingness."

The truth was that Isabelle did love Harriet very much, but she felt it more deeply when Harriet didn't rush in and ruin the moment with her normal criticisms or unnecessary details and useless advice. Harriet had a way of taking tender moments and destroying them. Harriet didn't know when to stop talking and as such, in her desire to fill every second of silence with chatter, she frequently said too much, and what she said unintentionally came out not at all how she intended. Harriet had a clean heart. Her motives were pure and in her heart of hearts she felt her advice to be more helpful than it actually was.

"I'm trying to help you but you don't want my help. I don't doubt your love for me. What I can't understand is why you don't like me the way I am." Harriet seemed almost hurt by Isabelle's profound declaration of love. "My experience is what I have achieved in life. My advice is, I think, the best gift I can give you. When you don't want to hear what I have to say, I feel like you are rejecting me," Harriet said more matter-of-fact than her normal communication pattern would lend.

Isabelle hadn't considered that by rejecting the advice that often felt like daggers directed at her most vulnerable places, she was making Harriet feel as though she was rejecting her personally. *How could this divide ever be bridged? How could she embrace the same words that had hurt her all these years?* She knew in her core that if she just absorbed everything her aunt hurled at her, it would continue to erode her confidence and self-worth even more than it already had been eroded by life. When she shielded it, she unintentionally made her aunt feel rejected, which further gnarled their relationship. How could Isabelle unearth a way to protect herself and still make her aunt feel validated?

At the hospital, Isabelle stopped at the nurses station in the ICU. The nursing supervisor informed her that Harriet had been taken for a less invasive procedure in a cath lab where a coil was inserted through her groin to the blood vessels in her brain to close off the aneurysm. But since the aneurysm was too big, she had to be prepped for emergency brain surgery. It all sounded so scary to Isabelle. She texted Carrie to see if she was working, and if she could meet for a cup of coffee on her break. Isabelle relied on Carrie for both emotional support as well as help navigating the system.

Isabelle walked into Harriet's dark, empty hospital room and relaxed into the firm leather recliner. She closed her eyes and leaned her head back.

"Hello." A voice interrupted. "I'm Liberty with case management. Are you Harriet Zelner's daughter?" The lady walked into the room like she was at home there.

"I'm Isabelle."

"Oh good. I was sent to talk to Mrs. Zelner's children about her progress," Liberty said.

"I'm who you're looking for."

"Yes, my list includes Isabelle, Zachary and Carrie. Oh, your sister is one of our ER doctors. Dr. Hoyt is highly respected," the nurse said with a jolly yet sincere laugh. "She took care of my daughter when she broke her arm last summer at day camp. She was walking down the boat ramp like she had done a thousand times." The nurse continued to talk but Isabelle tuned her out, to the point she didn't even realize the nurse had stopped talking. *Another old rambling lady.* "Isn't that something?" the nurse asked. Isabelle looked at her with a genuinely blank stare.

Isabelle was not amused. She didn't intend to appear annoyed, but she realized she must have come across that way when the case manager started slowly stepping backward toward the door. "Is this a good time? I can come back."

Carrie is not my sister. Isabelle hoped what she was thinking wasn't written across her face. Isabelle knew she needed to behave more graciously than she was feeling. She appreciated Carrie's dedication to Harriet, but hearing this brought up her long-held insecurities about how Carrie was the daughter Harriet really wanted.

"This is as good of a time as any," Isabelle said. "Carrie is like a sister but she's not actually," Isabelle clarified.

Sensing tension, the nurse's eyes narrowed in sympathy, and she sat down on the side of the bed. "I can remove her from the list if you like," she offered.

"No. No." Isabelle paused before she relented and filled in the blanks. "We do sort of have a sibling rivalry, I suppose. Her version of misbehaving was changing majors from physical therapy to pharmacy to medical school." Isabelle laughed nervously.

"I have a biological sister like that." Liberty offered this information clearly working to forge a bond with Isabelle, and it worked. "She always did everything right," Liberty added in a way that would draw more information out of Isabelle. "I used to call my sister pollywog, but really it was my own code name for Pollyanna." *She really did understand.*

"I used to call Carrie apothecary," Isabelle said laughing. "Look, it's silly. Carrie is awesome. She's great to Harriet, and she's truly family to Zach and me. My misgivings are stupid. Please don't mention this to anyone," Isabelle conceded. Just then, Isabelle's phone buzzed. It was a text from Carrie. "Ha!" Isabelle's eyes got big as she found irony in the timing. She held the phone around so Liberty could see that it was Carrie responding to the text Isabelle had sent just before the case manager showed up.

Carrie texted that she was at a conference in Seattle. Isabelle was disappointed. She was looking forward to coffee, but texted back a joke to keep things light, followed by her signature smiley face.

"Would you like to talk about Harriet's progress now or would it be better to wait until your brother can join you?" Liberty asked more confidently now that they had developed rapport.

"Oh, we tag team things. We can go over it and I will fill him in later," Isabelle said. "I'll fill Carrie in later as well. I didn't mean to imply that she isn't welcome in these discussions. She's usually the one advising us on what the test results actually mean."

"Very well," Liberty said as she opened her green notebook and talked about what Harriet likely needed and what Medicare would cover. "I see she has a supplement. That's good," she added.

Dealing with Harriet's health issues increased Isabelle's resolve to maintain her health through solid lifestyle choices. She didn't want this to be her thirty years from now.

When the discussion was over, Liberty extended one more offer on her way out the door. "If you ever need to talk, I'm a good listener." Isabelle appreciated that. It wasn't in her nature to look up a virtual stranger to listen to her talk, but she genuinely appreciated the offer.

After Liberty left, Isabelle relaxed a few more minutes with her eyes closed in the oversized leather recliner. There was so much she knew she should be doing but she felt too overwhelmed to know where to begin. She hoped Harriet's spirit would visit with an update.

Isabelle looked around for Harriet but of course she wasn't there. She was in surgery. *How amazing that Harriet met me at the gym to alert me to get to the hospital.*

Isabelle wouldn't have known to go otherwise. While she waited for Harriet to come out of surgery, Isabelle decided to get a coffee and call Zach.

Downstairs in the café, Isabelle perused the ornately displayed salad bar, which she surmised looked more like a country club Sunday buffet than what she considered to be standard hospital food. Oddly enough, this meticulously designed café presentation increased her confidence in the care she knew her aunt was receiving upstairs. There were a variety of a la carte items along with premade salad options, and she loved that each one was presented with a list of ingredients and health information per serving.

Remembering she hadn't yet eaten, Isabelle picked up a tray and small salad plate and began to choose a colorful assortment of fresh vegetables along with slices of hardboiled egg. For dressing she mixed her usual, a drizzle of olive oil followed by a healthy dose of vinegar. If there had been anyone else around, she would have told them that she always puts the oil on first to give the vinegar something to stick to. Isabelle loved what she considered to be teaching moments, even when she wasn't asked. But there was no one to teach, so she merely thought it and moved over to the line of drip coffee options before heading toward the register to pay. As she took her phone from her purse to call Zach, she looked up and saw him sitting in the courtyard. Without missing a step, she set the phone on the tray, paid for her meal, picked up silverware and a few napkins, and headed outside. He saw her coming and waved.

"I was just going to call you," Isabelle said as she set her tray on the table and sat down. "How did you know to come?"

"I was here two hours ago and haven't made it upstairs," Zach said. "I got summonsed to a conference call with a client that is looking to pull their account and go with a competitor."

"I'm sorry," Isabelle said.

"I'm not. They're a pain in the butt and the yield is so low that most months we don't make anything off them anyway. The boss can't see we're barely breaking even, and now it's going to be worse because he promised them the damn moon just to keep their portfolio," Zach said shaking his head back and forth. "I'm going to be running all over the place to do this and do that and if they don't get what they want they'll be calling Richard personally. I'd like to give Richard the account."

You could wrap it with a bow, and a note: 'Dear Dick,'" Isabelle laughed. She could be funny at times, but since it didn't happen often, it always caught Zach off guard.

"Awe. The old Izz is back, nice," Zach said. This put a satisfied look on her face.

"So you didn't know Harriet was in surgery?" Isabelle questioned.

"Surgery? Whatever for? I thought they were sending her to the cath lab this morning for a relatively common procedure," Zach said.

"They did but they couldn't close off the aneurysm so she's in surgery to place a clip to close it off," Isabelle clarified. Zach nodded as he silently listened.

"Do you ever wonder how our lives got here?" Zach asked his sister philosophically out of the blue. For a moment he looked up at the sky and bit his lower lip, before shifting his focus to something across the courtyard. *Was he looking at something specific or just fixated on an inanimate object?* He had never come across to Isabelle as much of a deep thinker so she really didn't know how to respond.

"What do you mean?" she asked, fidgeting with the zipper on her jacket.

"Well, look at us. Both alone. I guess you have a kid. No parents. Last living relative probably going to die soon. Workaholics. No real friends to speak of. What happened to us?" Zach asked.

"Our parents died," she said without missing a beat, as if it were obvious, and as if those three words on their own explained everything. "Plus, we do have friends. We have Carrie," Isabelle added, trying to lighten the conversation. *Carrie who I almost disowned to the case manager a half an hour ago.* Isabelle wasn't going to mention that part to Zach.

"She works more than we do. When isn't she on call or in the ER?" Zach asked.

"Well, she's not on call right now. She's in Seattle." Isabelle said this in a slightly competitive way to almost one-up Zach for not knowing this. "Besides, I have friends at work. I'm having drinks with them tonight. And you have had a lot of girlfriends. And Arnie is family. We're not completely alone in this world," she continued to defend their lives, pausing between each staccato sentence, each offered as one thought at a time.

"Yeah but we had Harriet and Frank; we had cousins on Frank's side we grew up with but it's like none of them care or come around. For all the boards and committees Harriet served on for years, none of these women have even tried to check how she's doing. Aren't chicks supposed to do stuff like that?" Zach asked.

"Well, I think most of the chicks that Harriet hung out with are dead, so no, they wouldn't be calling. Although…" Isabelle paused before finishing her thought. Surely she shouldn't tell Zach about her visits from Harriet.

"Although what?"

"Well, I mean, surely there's still staff at the organizations she volunteered for who would want to pay their respects. You'd think they would call. I don't know." Isabelle covered her tracks. She wasn't sure how Zach would handle the news of her visits, and they had become too important to her to risk having him make a joke of it. "Do you remember mom and dad?"

"I remember mom more than dad. Dad was gone a lot, except weekends when he worked in the yard," Zach said.

"Harriet didn't seem to think dad had much knowledge about growing anything, so it's odd that he worked in the yard," Isabelle said.

"I don't know that he grew anything. He cut the grass. Don't you remember him staining the picnic table every summer? We were told to stay away and not touch it until it dried. Remember that time I sat on the bench that he had just stained and it was still wet? I got my ass chewed. Not to mention stain all over my clothes."

"Where was I?" Isabelle asked.

"I don't know. You were younger. Maybe you were with mom," Zach said. "No, she was there, because she helped me get changed. I don't know where you were,"

Isabelle had no recollection of that story. She longed to hear these stories. They made her both feel alive and fulfilled, and at the same time, jealous that Zach even had memories she knew nothing about. "Do you remember when they added the back patio for us to roller skate on and we got to put our hand-prints in the wet cement?" Zach asked, excited to remember a day he had completely forgotten until now.

"I remember that," Isabelle said excitedly. It felt good to her to remember something that was oddly mundane and yet possibly still lasting to this day – that is, if the patio was still there. After a bit of silence, Isabelle spoke back up. "What was mom like?" Isabelle asked, partly because she wanted to hear what Zach remembered, to compare it to what she believed, and partly because she craved stories about Joy.

"Mom was pretty and funny. She made people laugh. It's probably where I got my charm," Zach said, nodding.

"Charm? Hmm. That's what you're calling it," Isabelle joked.

"She'd be all nice one minute and then just kinda called things like she saw it the next. But boy, she got things done. No one got in her way when there was something she wanted," he said.

"You were ten when they died. How did you pick up on that?"

"I don't know." Zach shrugged.

"What was she like with dad?" Isabelle inquired. Zach looked at her like he didn't understand what his sister was asking. "Did they get along? Was mom sarcastic around him?"

"I don't know. Harriet and grandma used to say mom was naughty-nice. Nice on the outside but willing to do whatever it took to get her way. Why all these weird questions all of a sudden? Where is this coming from?"

Isabelle didn't answer his question. "I'd like to be that way, funny and wry," Isabelle mused. "When I try to be, Arnie accuses me of being mad. Me? Mad?"

It was all Zach could do to keep from laughing. He knew better than to touch that statement with a fifty foot pole. He quickly redirected the subject back to their folks. "Dad talked about all kinds of things we were going to do or he was going to do. But when mom said she was going to do something, it was done the next day. Do you remember that tree house we had in the backyard?"

"Over the garden – red, yes." Isabelle was excited to again bring back another detail she had completely forgotten.

"Dad was going to build it on the other side of the yard, over by the tin shed. He sketched it out and started bringing home wood. Months went by. One afternoon, grandma and grandpa came over and grandpa and mom built it."

"Where was I?" Isabelle asked.

"You were probably playing dolls with grandma," Zach said without hesitation. "Mom later told me she wanted to have it where she could watch us from her garden. She said it wouldn't have made sense to have it across the yard where dad was going to put it. Isn't that crazy?" Zach asked, mostly with admiration.

"It's sort of calculating in both a nice and naughty way," Isabelle observed.

"Probably where naughty-nice came from," Zach said as he lifted and lowered his eyebrows. "Mom went about things her own way and got what she wanted without rocking the boat too much," Zach paused before adding, "Amone is like that. It's why I'm going to ask her to marry me."

"What? Marry you? Because she's manipulative? Not to mention cold." Isabelle wanted to throw up a little in her mouth. She could barely stomach Amone, and now Zach wanted to make them sisters. *No wonder I don't have an appetite.*

"You see Amone as cold and aloof but that's not how she is with me. You want her to kiss your ass," Zach surmised.

"No!" Isabelle interrupted. "I want her to be polite. Engaging. Personable. I want her to acknowledge me when she walks in and I'm there or when I walk into a room."

"That's not a deal breaker for me. But I'll talk to her. See if I can encourage her to warm up to you," Zach promised.

"You don't need to talk to her for me," Isabelle interjected.

"Plus, she's sexy as hell," Zach said with a grin.

"That's a great reason to marry someone," Isabelle said sarcastically while she nodded. "Do you think that's her stripper name? Isabelle asked, intentionally mispronouncing her name.

"It's Amone. Like Amore, only with an "N". You know. Love." Zach smiled as he said this. This cued Isabelle to roll her eyes. "Women are always judging other women based on how well they fit into a chick click. Dudes don't care about that."

"You should. Women are the glue of the relationship," Isabelle started before Zach interrupted.

"You make things sticky?" Always the prankster, Zach cracked himself up.

"We hold families together, schedules and social circles together. You need someone who's human enough to connect with others." Isabelle was trying to mother her brother but he had already made up his mind.

71

"I don't care anything about that. I want a woman who's loving, who listens to me and who cares about me – and lets me care about her in my own way," Zach started. "Someone who wants to spend time with me but doesn't freak out if I'm working or don't call her for a few days. Amone is gorgeous. She smells good. She likes sex, and we have fun," Zach concluded.

"Fun doesn't pay the bills. Nor does sexy," Isabelle stated matter-of-fact.

"I want what you have," Zach said. "A family. Is that such a terrible thing?"

"First of all, you have a family. And secondly, I'm not sure how much of a family Arnie and I are going to be. He moved out. We fight all the time. Nothing I do is right or good enough. You've heard him correct me like all the time. Oh – and I recently found out he kissed another woman."

"What? Did you see him?" Zach asked

"No. I don't care. I do care, but I shouldn't. We're separated."

"Listen, Arnie is not perfect, and my loyalty is to you first. But despite your problems, that man loves you. I don't know where you got your information, but I don't believe it," Zach was adamant.

"I heard it from the horse's mouth."

"He told you he kissed another woman?" Zach was clearly in disbelief.

"No, his new ho. I work with her." *Did I really just call her that? Yes, I did!*

"You should probably hear his side before you get too excited."

"I'm not going to ask him about it. We're separated," Isabelle repeated as if Zach didn't know.

"Mom used to say, 'Like water off a duck' whenever dad would do something that would push her buttons. There's no such thing as a perfect relationship – I should know. I've had a lot of them. But I guess I've learned that you have to listen to the patterns and pick your battles," Zach said.

Wouldn't kissing someone else be something worth paying attention to? And who says they stopped at kissing?

"You're the last person I ever thought I'd be taking relationship advice from," Isabelle admitted. But she had to wonder if Zach wasn't actually on to something. She thought about some of the arguments with Arnie, and she did let everything he said get under her skin.

When it was just them, it was easier to let the little things go.

But once Grace came along, Isabelle needed him to stop being the playful parent and start backing her up – a role he refused to embrace. If anything, he became more childlike and wasteful after Grace came along and it was up to Isabelle to single-handedly maintain order in the home. *He did this to me.*

Was it so bad that Isabelle wanted to instill healthy habits at home to set a good example for Grace? Was it so wrong that she refused to let him speed and reminded him to drive safely to keep their daughter safe? Was it unfair for her to track the progress on the goals they outlined and prioritized together? It wasn't as if she had just given him a list. They made the list together, and he was the one who always let her down. Was it so bad to hate being corrected on everything she said, even when she was right and on things he knew nothing about? Was she really so bad because she didn't want to feel invisible and like nothing she wanted mattered? That's how Arnie made her feel. Everything she did, she did for the family, for the home, and for the life she was under the impression they were building together.

73

Isabelle decided that maybe there could be value in reconsidering her separation from Arnie – unless he really had moved on to someone new. Maybe she would talk to him and give him a chance to convince her that there was hope for him moving back in. Certainly it was something she knew Grace would want. She wouldn't promise herself anything concrete, beyond the fact that she was willing to at least hear him out one last time.

She couldn't believe Zach was marrying Amone. Isabelle had just about nailed her impression of the woman she hoped would be moving on soon, but now appeared might be sticking around. Zach had never talked about marrying any of his past girlfriends. *Sexy as hell? Yep, leave it to Zach to marry the girl with the red stiletto heels.*

"Do you have Grace tonight?" Zach asked.

"No, she's with Arnie. Why?"

"I thought you might go with me to give me your opinion on rings for Amone," Zach's eyebrows went up as he asked.

"You're serious about this," Isabelle said. "Have you even asked her what she wants in terms of a ring?"

"I thought I'd make it a surprise," Zach said confidently.

"Traditional male thinking. Arnie bought me a yellow gold engagement ring. I don't even like yellow gold. I would have picked white gold or platinum. We couldn't have afforded platinum. But he never even asked. I think you should ask her what she likes before you spend several months pay," Isabelle said.

"Several months? I'm going to a diamond discounter. I figured five thousand dollars should more than cover it," Zach said.

"I guess."

"You guess?" Zach was probing.

"I guess if I saw the two of you and you appeared to be madly in love, then honestly a band and a decent stone would probably make her happy. Because saying yes would be about spending her life with you, not the diamond you were buying her. But she seems showier than that. What if you started with a promise ring or a commitment ring? What if you took some time to get to know her, so you would know what she wanted? Men make all these grand gestures without ever listening to what matters to us and then you're disappointed when we don't squeal like baby pigs when you do something quote-unquote romantic," Isabelle scolded.

"Are you saying that to me or is this something you wished you could say to Arnie? Cause it sounds like you have a different audience in mind given your tone," Zach observed.

"I'm going to let some of that stuff go with Arnie. You were right. I guess I probably bust his chops too much over stuff that doesn't really matter," Isabelle conceded. "I was planning to get together with some friends tonight but maybe I'll call him and see if he wants to bring Grace and have dinner together. That might be a good first step."

Isabelle was proud of herself for coming to this decision, even if it wasn't a decision she came to on her own. "Now see, I would prefer to text but since he doesn't text and prefers to call, I'm being flexible," Isabelle joked as she dialed the phone. It went to voicemail so Isabelle left him a message: "Thought I'd see if you and Grace want to have dinner with me. I have plans but I'd rather spend the evening with you two. Call me." Isabelle was confident this would make his day.

"So I guess ring shopping with me is out?" Zach joked.

"My heart wouldn't be in it," Isabelle said. She knew, deep down, this was selfish, but in the moment she didn't care.

Isabelle cleared her dishes to the bin and she and Zach walked upstairs to the ICU together. *Maybe things will work out after all. Harriet will get better. Zach and I will get along again – and Arnie will move back in.* The sun was coming back out in her world. All this doom and gloom was unfounded. Life may have handed her some lemons lately but she was ready to roll up her sleeves and squeeze some lemonade.

Isabelle was not a praying person, but her daughter was. Praying before meals and bed was one of those rituals Arnie had taught her. Isabelle wasn't opposed to it, although she also didn't encourage it. *Wouldn't it be crazy if there is a God and He heard Grace's miracle prayer? I guess anything is possible.*

Just then a text came in. It was from Arnie. "Enjoy dinner with the girls. Grace and I are catching a movie tonight. See you tomorrow. I have something for you." This was practically a book for Arnie. "I have something for you," Isabelle read Arnie's text to Zach and emphasized this last line. "Maybe your advice came at the right time," Isabelle told her brother. "He's going to have to make some effort too but this could be a good first step," she said smiling.

"I hope so," Zach said, throwing his arm around his sister's shoulder and squeezing her.

At the ICU, the nursing supervisor informed the siblings of complications with the surgery. Harriet was still in the operating room. It would be hours until she was in recovery. Then it could be hours until she was returned to the ICU. It seemed to Isabelle and Zach that they should just head out for the night and call the other when either of them heard news.

Isabelle was looking forward to dinner and drinks out with some women from her office, even though she only really knew one of them. It had been a long time since she dressed up, but things were looking up and she was eager to begin a fresh new chapter.

CHAPTER 5

Isabelle checked her lipstick in her rearview mirror before pulling ahead for the valet. She felt confident in her snakeskin Jimmy Choo shoes and black leather miniskirt. She winked at the valet as she got out of her Lexus IS C 250. "Be sure to smile for my dash cam," she said, leaning over the open window of her convertible, and pausing an extra beat before adding, "I want to be able to enjoy your dimples again tomorrow."

Isabelle did not have a camera hidden in her dash. But she had heard horror stories of valet drivers taking sports cars for test drives, and sometimes pilfering through consoles. So she generally tried to make some sort of flirty comment intended to scare them just enough into treating her car the same way they would if she were riding shotgun. And it worked. They never even took the loose change she left pooled in plain sight.

Some women from her office had a table waiting, with a purse holding a solitary chair for Isabelle when she walked into the packed pub. She wasn't sure everyone at the table was a friend. She specifically had her suspicions about Tina, after her unexpected confession that Arnie had kissed her. *Who invited her?* It seemed like an innocent misunderstanding, but Isabelle's intuition made the hair stand up on her arm.

Stop over-thinking everything. Just have fun tonight.

Isabelle didn't go out that often after dark anymore and

forgot there was an entire community that came alive after nine o'clock. "I ordered for you," her friend Sabra leaned in to say, practically yelling it to be heard over the music and roar of the crowd.

Just as Isabelle mouthed the words "thank you" her martini arrived, complete with two olives, just the way she liked it. Isabelle pointed to the two olives and mouthed to Sabra, "How did you know?"

Sabra also had a martini, only she had already downed her olives, leaving just a blue plastic toothpick behind. "I ordered my favorite and told the server to make it two."

"Good choice. Thank you," Isabelle smiled and nodded.

Almost everyone struggled to hear or share any semblance of real conversation. As such, most of the chit-chat was superficial and consisted of questions and answers that could be exchanged with just a few words. Fortunately for Isabelle, an ear infection that left her hard of hearing as a child also led her to develop the sometimes useful skill of reading lips.

She paid particular attention when she noticed the intrusive and possibly iniquitous Tina, across the table, mouth Arnie's name.

Oh no she's not. She's talking about my husband to someone we work with. Isabelle was fuming.

If this was a genuine misunderstanding, Isabelle couldn't understand why Tina would be talking about it to anyone other than her. She wanted to confront her, but she didn't want to seem paranoid, jealous or crazy when it could have been a different Arnie altogether.

Plus, she wasn't intoxicated enough to bring her inhibitions down that far, and in a room this loud, she had no intention of getting to that point. It was eating her up enough that when Sabra leaned in to share a funny story, all Isabelle could focus on was the conversation that wasn't directed at her. She struggled to balance her frustration with an appearance of congeniality.

Faking it was not her forte, so when a stranger walked up and asked her to dance, she immediately accepted. Even if her feet hurt tomorrow, she knew it was better than saying something she regretted tonight.

A few dances and Isabelle was ready to head home. She didn't feel like eating anything. She looked forward to reuniting with Arnie, resolving whatever differences they had, and getting this whole matter with Tina out in the open where they could deal with it like adults. She was fully ready to put an end to this charade of a night life. Isabelle much preferred the comfort of a night at home with Arnie and Grace.

While Isabelle was happy to seem hip to her younger co-workers, she was a homebody at heart. She preferred yoga pants to heels any night that didn't involve a cozy dinner out with Arnie, and frankly it had been a very long time since she could remember one of those.

◆ ◆ ◆

Isabelle loved Saturdays, especially selfish Saturdays when Grace was with Arnie. She delighted in the fantasy of being back together with Arnie, but she also recognized a part of her would miss these little jewels of time she had exclusively to herself. Isabelle considered herself a morning person, despite the fact that she always struggled to get to her nine o'clock yoga class on time.

Her sleepy Saturdays usually started before seven, when she flipped the news on with the television remote, and only took a break long enough to scoot out to the kitchen and brew a cup of coffee in her Keurig. It was a particularly good day when she opened the refrigerator to find fresh half and half for her coffee. If it wasn't fresh or there wasn't enough of it, Isabelle took her coffee black. It was one of many ways she was discriminating in her preferences.

On this particular Saturday, coffee in hand, Isabelle headed back to bed to snuggle in and flip through a series of news channels to find out what she missed going on in the world. Between Harriet's stroke and her relationship with Arnie coming to a head, it felt like forever since she indulged in the luxury of digesting a whole hour of news in one sitting.

Her cell phone buzzed on the nightstand. The text was from Arnie. Seeing his name made her smile as she anticipated the day ahead with him and Grace. "Noon at Abby's?"

Her old self would have criticized his choice of a pizzeria, but her new, intentionally more relaxed and less critical self responded, "Sounds great. I love their salad bar." But before she hit send, she wanted to rethink this. Did she sound rigid? Did her message sound critical as if all she would approve of was the salad bar? Was there a chance this could inspire him to shake his head or squint his eyes – which was basically how she knew she had managed to get under his skin, and not in a good way? Isabelle erased what she wrote and typed instead, "Sounds great. See you soon." She hit send. Yes, that was a better option. She was finally determined to actively participate in putting their marriage back together even if it meant biting her tongue eighty percent of the time.

After yoga, Isabelle showered and selected one of Arnie's favorite outfits. He always loved her legs so she picked out a casual skirt she could wear with some ornately decorated flip flops. When she stepped outside she was suddenly snapped back to the reality of fall in the Northwest. It was clearly too cold for flip flops and might even be too cold for bare legs. She changed her shoes and powered through the chill in the autumn air. She wasn't the first woman to suffer discomfort to look her best for a man.

When Isabelle arrived at the pizzeria, Arnie was waiting in the lobby. He was wearing her favorite blue shirt; she bought it for him two Christmases ago and she loved the way it complemented his coloring. He was smiling in a relaxed way she hadn't seen from him in a long time. He stood up when she walked through the door and came over to greet her with an encompassing hug and a deep sigh, she assumed of relief. When he asked how she was doing, she felt as if he really cared. So many times over the past year they both said things for the sake of saying them, or asked questions of each other that seemed irrelevant. Just as she was changing, Isabelle could tell that Arnie had also changed. He was no longer going through the motions and this gave her great hope.

"Where's Grace?" Isabelle asked.

"Her friend Lisa called to see if she could spend the afternoon so I let her go," Arnie said.

And you didn't bother to ask me?

Isabelle resisted the urge to get upset. If she was going to make this work there would be times she would have to do so on a moment-by-moment basis and this was one of them. "So, what should we get on our pizza?"

"You're having pizza?" Arnie asked.

"If you don't mind the gluten free crust, I'll have whatever you're having." She smiled at him with the same flirty wink she gave the valet driver the night before. *Could two times be a charm?*

"Who are you?" Arnie asked and laughed at the same time.

"Look, I'm trying. I'm trying to be easier and breezier. I'm making an effort," she told Arnie.

He inhaled slowly and exhaled mindfully. "Me too," he said. Isabelle smiled, but for the first time she worried that maybe making things work with Arnie wouldn't be the easy task she had convinced herself over the last twenty-four hours. Arnie kissed her on the forehead and walked over to order. "Do you want a salad?" he turned around to ask.

"Yes, a small, please," she answered.

The restaurant was crowded but not noisy like the pub the night before. It was mostly families and couples out for a Saturday lunch.

"How's Harriet doing?" Arnie asked.

"Zach called this morning. She came out of surgery and is stabilized. But she's still in ICU. I need to stop in and see her today." She paused. "I probably do need to start working on her eulogy." She desperately wanted to tell Arnie about these unorthodox visits they had been having since her stroke, but she chose to hold onto that information for now.

"I know you'll do right by her," Arnie said.

"It's not like we've ever been close or really even connected until recently. I mean, I know she always loved Zach and me, but I never really felt like she truly accepted me. It's like she wanted me to be different or maybe she resented that she had to raise her sister's kids and never had her own. I don't know," Isabelle said. Isabelle had to be careful talking too much about this with Arnie. She didn't want to poison the great vibe they had going. He wasn't a particularly deep man. She and Arnie connected best when they were doing something physical together much more so than having a philosophical conversation about the meaning of life.

She also wanted to bring up the subject of Tina, but decided that too might be enough to turn a good conversation sour.

"So you had fun last night?" Arnie said, half a question, half observation.

"Not really. It was ok. Loud. Boring. I would have rather been home with you and Grace." Isabelle shrugged.

Arnie pulled out his phone and handed it to her. On it, she saw a picture.

Suddenly and with a jolt, everything in Isabelle's world stopped. There was no sound. No movement. It was as if he and she and the picture on the phone were frozen in time. Isabelle almost forgot to even breathe. Her mouth dropped silently open in complete disbelief. Images flashed through her mind like an old film reel running frame by frame in slow motion.

As slow as each second seemed to pass, the urgency of the moment was not unlike the sensation of her complete world hurling out of control in slow but inevitable motion, as if she were trapped in a car that had just left a bridge headed for a lake. She couldn't feel her fingers or her toes. Even her mind and her words were stilled. This was not just any picture on Arnie's phone. *What was happening? Who would do this and why?*

CHAPTER 6

"**S**o I danced with a guy at a bar. I don't even know his name. Who sent this to you anyway?" Isabelle demanded to know.

"Does it matter?" Arnie fired back. "To be honest, it was nice to see you out having fun and not so uptight."

Isabelle scrolled back in Arnie's phone to read the text that accompanied the picture that signaled once and for all that everything had indeed already changed. It was from the now notorious Tina, who up until a couple of days ago Isabelle had never even noticed.

The audacity of this bitch. Pretending to be concerned that my husband kissed her, then talking about him at girls' night, and now, sending a photo of me dancing with a stranger to him?

It wasn't so much the picture that alarmed Isabelle, as much as what it signified, and the text that preceded it. The message from Tina said, "You can see Izz is fine. She's moving on." Only Zach and Arnie referred to Isabelle by the casual nickname. Her co-worker had to have picked it up from one of them, and Tina had never met Zach.

Arnie talked to Tina about us. About me.

"Why is Tina texting you about me? Do you talk to other women about us?" As Isabelle asked the question, the answer suddenly hit her.

Before Arnie could even answer, she hit him where it hurt. "She paid a visit to my office this week and told me you kissed her. She said she thought you were my brother since we have the same last name."

"There's no way she thought that," Arnie said.

"She sat in my office, encouraging me to talk to her. She's quite an actress."

Isabelle couldn't tell if Arnie felt shame or surprise by the look on his face.

"How does she even have your number? She's my co-worker." Isabelle stopped cold.

"We're like friends, I guess. It's not what you think," Arnie said.

"What do you think I think?" Isabelle raised her voice. Isabelle was suddenly aware of the people around them and realized that Arnie had this all planned out. Grace was mysteriously with a friend, and they were having lunch in a crowded place. *None of this was by accident.*

"I met her at the gym. You and I were on a break. It's not the big thing I know you're going to make this into, but we are separated," Arnie pointed out.

"Wow," Isabelle mouthed nodding. None of this seemed possible. Isabelle didn't see any of it coming. She had been working so hard to find a way to create a second chance for her and Arnie and all the while he had moved on with someone Isabelle had to see and work with every day. "I honestly came here today thinking we were going to give our marriage a second chance. I never imagined you would tell me you were seeing someone else and all the hopes we had, or our daughter had to reconcile had vanished." Isabelle was cut off by another declaration by Arnie.

"I've already talked to Grace," he said.

"Of course you have. You wouldn't involve me in that conversation. I'm only her mother. Maybe you had Tina there?"

"No, it was just Grace and me. And I told her that part of life is accepting that people change and life changes and we learn to accept those changes and adapt to those changes, sometimes better than other times," he said.

You are such a jackass, Arnie.

Isabelle sat staring off into the crowd of people that filled the restaurant, only half listening while Arnie rambled. Her right elbow rested on the table and she moved her hand so that it now covered her forehead and her eyes. Never in a million years would she have predicted this when she woke up and left the house this morning.

Finally she spoke, "I don't know what happened. How did we get here? Earlier this week you wanted to move back in. Yesterday, you had a gift for me and today you're showing me a stupid picture and telling me you're seeing one of my co-workers. What the hell happened?" she asked.

Arnie could have easily cleared the situation about Tina up with one simple statement, "I'm not seeing her." But he didn't.

"I know you're trying. I appreciate that, really I do. But Izz, I've been unhappy for a long time. And I just got tired of pretending. You're a wonderful woman – just not for me anymore," he said. He knew his words hit her like bricks. He didn't want to hurt her but he had thought about this for months and there was no way around it. He even second-guessed himself, considering a change of mind. He thought about moving back in. But the truth was, he was miserable. She was miserable, and as much as they loved each other and their daughter, their marriage was no longer the safe harbor it once was. There was so much more he could have told her, but there was no point. He could see it would only hurt her and he didn't want to hurt her more than he already had.

"You didn't have a gift for me?" she asked.

"A gift?" Arnie questioned.

"Yesterday you said you had a gift for me, but you didn't have a gift," she said.

"No, I said I had something for you, not a gift," he clarified.

"No, clearly, not a gift," Isabelle said. It pained him to do this but Arnie pulled an envelope out of his pocket. Inside was a copy of the petition and summons for divorce. Isabelle unfolded the papers and read them aloud to Arnie, "The petitioner has started an action in the above court requesting that your marriage be dissolved. Additional requests if any are stated in the petition." She stopped and set them down on the table. "You have great timing, Arnie. Harriet could be gone any day and now you're divorcing me. This is just great," she said as she folded the papers up and stuffed them in her purse.

As she stood up, he stopped her with one more agonizing request. "I need to have you sign this acceptance of service as proof you received these papers," he said.

I'll give you proof!

"You are such a coward. You set this whole thing up," she said as she leaned down and signed the paper he presented. "I can't believe I ever loved you." She threw the pen at him, turned and walked away to leave. He flinched when the pen hit him but he accepted the hit as a minor sting compared to what he knew she must be feeling. He wanted to run after her, hug her and tell her they could still be friends. But he knew this was not the time.

When Isabelle arrived at her car, she sat in the driver's seat, dropped her face into her hands and began to weep. She had heard of people hitting bottom, but she always thought of it as an anecdote of having a really bad day. Now she knew that hitting bottom was that precise moment of decision, when all hope seemed lost, where she would give up and stop breathing entirely or somehow summon the strength to march forward despite the odds.

She felt as if her heart was physically breaking, as if her heart as an organ had physiologically lost the ability to pump blood anymore. *How could such a great morning turn into such a nightmare of a day?*

CHAPTER 7

When she finally cried all the tears her eyes could possibly cry, she decided to drive with no destination in mind. A couple hours later, and completely by surprise, Isabelle found herself at Rosie's – best known for their milkshakes. *I don't drink these. What am I doing here?*

Isabelle knew exactly what she was doing here. She had to use the bathroom and she couldn't just use the facilities and leave without buying something. Anything. She parked and walked in where she was immediately greeted by a hostess wearing a teal and white striped shirt. Classic rock was playing through the speakers. *Zach would love this place.*

Isabelle was seated in one of about ten shiny leather booths that circled the dining area. It was very old school. Letter board menus hung on the walls. The salt and pepper shakers on each table had old fashioned pictures of fruit on them. *Apples, pears and pansies. Interesting combination.* She decided to opt for a simple scoop of ice cream. The place seemed more Jersey Shore than Northeast Portland. She was happy to read that the chocolate chip mint ice cream was gluten free.

Her server's name was Harriet. *How ironic.* Unlike her aunt, this Harriet was almost as round as she was tall, and had big, bright red curls, that reminded Isabelle of a grown-up Raggedy Ann doll. She wore bright red lipstick and thick black mascara. She was very nice.

"You sure you want ice cream? It's good but the extra rich milkshake has a higher butterfat content that makes it super creamy and utterly divine," the server named Harriet said. Isabelle supposed that might sound enticing to someone else, but it just sounded like a lot of extra calories to her.

"A scoop of chocolate chip mint will be perfect," Isabelle said.

"You just want a single?" Harriet asked again. "You can add a second scoop in anther flavor. We have banana nut, cotton candy, even bubblegum."

Mostly, Isabelle wanted to use the ladies room. Naturally, in her quest to access a bathroom, she found the friendliest, most talkative server she had ever run across. Harriet the server asked a lot of questions and rattled off a lot of information that Isabelle let enter one ear and slide right out the other. "I'm sorry to interrupt, but do you have a ladies room?" Isabelle was biting her lip.

"Oh Darlin', we sure do. It's in the back to the left."

"Fantastic," Isabelle said, grabbing her purse as she stood up to start walking that direction.

Isabelle needed to get away from everything. She wished this was a bad dream and she could just wake up. Maybe all of it was a dream – Harriet's stroke and Arnie serving her with divorce papers.

When she arrived back at her table, Harriet the server was just arriving with her single scoop of ice cream. "What brings you to Rosie's today?" Harriet the server asked.

"I was just driving around and had to use the bathroom," Isabelle confessed. Now that she was more comfortable, her chatty server didn't bother her quite so much.

"Out to clear your head?" the server asked.

"Yes, actually. How did you know?"

"You have that look about you," Harriet said. *What look is that?*

"I have a lot going on. Sometimes it just gets to be a bit much," Isabelle said.

"You should drive on out to the falls. Multnomah Falls. Little trails. Lots of water. It's only about twenty-five miles from here. Just head east on I-84."

Isabelle tried to imagine how much her server could possibly know about hiking the steep trails that led to Larch Mountain. *Did most people even know the trails extend beyond the footbridge?* "Maybe I will," Isabelle said.

"Good thing you ordered that ice cream for nourishment. Sure you don't want a second scoop?"

"I'm good. Thanks." Isabelle thoroughly enjoyed the entire scoop. It was the first dish of anything she enjoyed so much and devoured like she hadn't eaten in days – despite the fact she had eaten lunch only a couple hours before with Arnie. *That was amazing ice cream!* She left before the check came, but she left Harriet a ten dollar bill as a thank you for the kind words and great service. *Maybe I will drive to Multnomah Falls. Good suggestion, Harriet.*

The drive was beautiful with the last of the fall leaves waiting to be blown off the trees before winter. The sky was blue with white, fluffy cumulus clouds. Their choppy appearance, as irregular fragments of cotton that had been gently pulled apart, felt oddly whimsical.

Once when she and Zach were small, before the accident, their parents took them to the ice caves at Mt. Baker where Isabelle picked up a small gray and white rock that stayed perpetually cold, even when set in a hot, sunny window sill. The five-mile trail hike seemed like an enormous undertaking for a small child, but just when she was ready to quit, her dad scooped her into his arms and carried her the last while. After that, even after her parents died, Isabelle felt safe in nature. And even without her father to carry her the rest of the way, tackling trails was a way Isabelle could also overcome the less concrete mountains and challenges in her everyday life.

Isabelle parked in the lot and grabbed only her cell phone and a light windbreaker before heading out. Several hundred feet from the car she decided to go back and grab a water bottle. Whether she needed it or not, Isabelle was always prepared for an emergency.

As she closed the door to her car, a car pulled up in the spot directly beside her. When she looked over she recognized Amone. *Oh dang. Her.* Isabelle did a double-take to make sure, but yes indeed, it the driver certainly looked like that cold, willowy fish with whom her brother seemed smitten. Isabelle waved, not expecting a response. Amone appeared to be just as surprised to see Isabelle. *Be nice*, Isabelle reminded herself.

"Hi," Amone said first. Isabelle was surprised she recognized her, let alone spoke to her.

"Hi," Isabelle said back. *I guess there's no ignoring her now.*

"Are you meeting someone or just out hiking to clear your mind?" Amone asked.

Isabelle was tempted to count the words in that question and note it was probably more than her brother's girlfriend had ever spoken to her. But she didn't. Instead, she just answered her question, "Mostly to clear my head." Isabelle smiled.

"Me too," Amone said. Again Isabelle fought the urge to speak her mind and forcibly refrained from any sarcastic comments. "I guess we could hike together?" Amone suggested. That was the last thing Isabelle wanted, but there wasn't much she could do about that now. Isabelle nodded. The two women took off side-by-side, neither saying a word for the first quarter of a mile. While the silence was a bit awkward, just talking for the sake of it would have been more awkward, so they continued on the trail, both working things out silently in their own minds.

"I haven't been here in a while," Isabelle said, oddly struck by the inconvenient coincidence of arriving at the same exact place and practically the same time as Amone.

"I come here all the time. I like to get outside, smell the trees, and feel the dirt and rocks under my tennis shoes," Amone said. *Oh please. She's one of those girls.*

"Uncle Frank used to bring Zach and me out here to work off some energy, as Harriet would say," Isabelle said.

"That's awesome. My dad used to bring me here. My mom died when I was nine and it was just dad and me," Amone said.

"I'm sorry about your mom," Isabelle said.

"Thanks. It was awful. She was hit by a drunk driver."

Isabelle suddenly felt a kindred spirit with the woman she previously assumed she had nothing in common. *So she lost her mom as a little girl too.*

"Dad and I used to come here until about five or six years ago," Amone said.

"I'm sure it gets harder to hike these trails when folks get to a certain age." Isabelle didn't know exactly how old Amone was, but she guessed she was within six or seven years of Zach and her.

"He was diagnosed with lung cancer and gone within six months. One summer we were hiking and that Christmas he was gone. So I got a dog."

Isabelle didn't know what to say to that, so she said nothing. But she did reach out to put her hand on Amone's upper left arm as a show of support. Amone specifically turned to Isabelle, tipped her head to the right and smiled. *What more could possibly come out on this day of unexpected revelations?*

"I met Zach on this exact trail," Amone volunteered, raising her eyebrows. "Three years ago."

"Three years ago?" Isabelle half asked and half exclaimed. "I thought you met earlier this year."

"No, we met here, three years ago," Amone confirmed. Isabelle wondered why Zach had never mentioned her prior to a few months ago. He always seemed to be dating someone. Isabelle thought Amone was just one of the many girls who drifted in and out of his life.

"I had my dog with me. She was tired and had sprained her leg, but I didn't know it. I thought she just didn't want to walk. She was a big dog so she pretty much did what she wanted to do. There I was trying to prod this Dobie, that was 40 pounds lighter than me – but twice as strong – down a trail, and she was not complying," Amone continued.

"You don't still bring your dog with you?" Isabelle asked.

"No," Amone said reflectively. By her tone, Isabelle wondered for a moment if the dog had died.

"I'm sorry," Isabelle said. For the first time, Isabelle realized she may have completely misjudged this woman she had seen several times but never really talked to or heard speak.

"She's not my dog any more. So, this tall, blonde, gorgeous man walks up to me and instead of looking at me, beyond a quick initial glance, he was absolutely consumed with the well-being of Winnie. He asked me if she was okay, and before I could even answer he knelt down beside her and wrapped his large hands around her front leg she had been favoring," Amone said, smiling.

"Zach has always been an animal lover," Isabelle shared.

"I thought he was a veterinarian or something," Amone said. "Then he picked up my 75-pound Doberman pincer and carried her the rest of the way as if she was a big baby. I was pretty sure he was planning to hit on me, but he didn't. Even when we got to my car and he asked for my number, he only ever used it to call and check on my dog," Amone said.

"Wow. So what happened to Winnie?" Isabelle asked.

Isabelle never could have imagined her brother meeting a woman as beautiful as Amone and not making a move. Inwardly, she was a bit impressed to hear about this side of him. In fact, she was so taken back, she completely spaced over the fact that Zach also had a Doberman named Winnie.

"I started dating someone else and I moved in with him, only he didn't want Winnie. He said dogs were messy and inconvenient. Stupid me, I picked the man over Winnie," Amone said.

"So what happened to your dog?" Isabelle asked, too engrossed in the story to put the pieces unfolding in front of her together.

"I called the nice man who carried her down the trail," Amone gushed.

"Zach? Zach's dog was your dog?"

"Yep. I needed to find someone who I knew would take care of her," Amone said.

This was a turn Isabelle never expected – to hear about this side of Zach or see this side of Amone. "So I guess things didn't work out with the other guy?" Isabelle asked.

"Nope. He wasn't a nice guy. Never trust a man who doesn't like animals. I learned that the hard way – twice!" Amone said. "So I broke up with the other guy and called Zach to see if I could borrow Winnie. I wanted her back but I didn't think it was fair to ask him for that. So I asked if I could just borrow her for a weekend. I was sad and I missed my best friend."

"Then you returned the dog and started seeing my brother?" Isabelle asked.

"Nope. He had just started dating someone else. We were never anything but friends. We would get together periodically to do something together with Winnie, but it was really all about her. We were in a way like co-parents," Amone said. The time passed quickly and Isabelle was surprised to see how much ground they had covered on the trail.

"After a couple years, we were both single at the same time. Zach called to see if I wanted to meet him and Winnie for breakfast one Saturday out on the deck at Luna Café. After breakfast, back at the car, I hugged and kissed Winnie, hugged Zach, and out of nowhere he kissed me. Completely unexpected. I never thought he saw me that way. I jumped in his car and spent the day with him and Winnie. We've been together ever since." Amone told the story casually as if it were really nothing, but both women knew it was a whole lot more.

"So what did you come here to think about today?" Isabelle's question took Amone by surprise. "When I saw you, you said you come here when you need to think," Isabelle reminded her.

"I guess I'm wondering where I stand with your brother. I love him but I don't know if he feels the same. He never says it or really talks about the future much at all. I don't want to be one of the many women who just pass through, if you know what I mean," Amone confided.

"I'm certain you're not that," Isabelle smiled. For the first time, she could see a future where Amone was her sister, and for the first time she was pleasantly intrigued by that. "Give him some time and space. You may find he's closer than you think."

When the women got back to their cars, Isabelle noticed a gold chain Amone wore around her neck. "I like your chain. Was it a gift?" Isabelle asked.

"No, I bought it on vacation a few years back. I usually don't like yellow gold but this was just the perfect length to wear casually so I actually find myself wearing it a lot. Do you like it?" Amone asked.

"Yes, I like it quite a lot," Isabelle said before the women said goodbye and turned to walk toward their own cars.

"We could do this again sometime?" Amone hinted.

I can't believe we're actually going to be friends. "I'd like that," Isabelle said before she waved goodbye and closed the car door.

As Isabelle headed back the forty miles to Portland, she couldn't help but think that nothing about this day had turned out as she expected.

Grace was still with her friend and clearly things with Arnie had changed forever. After an afternoon of fact finding, Isabelle had a choice to make; and she chose to invest in the one relationship she felt confident she could save.

She drove up to Zach's estate to surprise him. Zach answered the door, surprised to see her. "Are you ok?" he asked. Winnie barked excitedly and came over to lick Isabelle's neck when she bent down to pet the dog.

"So you know about Arnie?" she asked.

"Yep, I'm sorry. Wanna join me out at the pool?" Isabelle loved his solar-heated saltwater pool on his terrace, and he knew it. "I'll get you some ice tea."

"Nope. Not today. Get dressed. You're coming with me," Isabelle said. "It's a surprise."

"Where are we going?" he asked.

"It's a surprise. Get dressed," she teasingly ordered her brother. He didn't question her orders given everything he knew she was going through. Winnie stayed with Isabelle while Zach went to change. Despite Isabelle's upbeat mood, he knew what was going on. It seemed Arnie talked to everyone close to

Isabelle before he actually gave Isabelle the news that their marriage was over.

Isabelle insisted on driving her car, which once again Zach agreed to. "Where are you taking me?" She didn't respond but instead put the top on the convertible down and turned the music up as she sped away, quite a bit faster than the posted neighborhood speed limit signs. "Whoa, slowdown cowgirl," Zach said.

Every time Zach tried to ask Isabelle a question over the music, she ignored him and sang along, sometimes making up her own words. "Those aren't actually the words," he would say, testing to see if she could hear him.

"They're my words," she would say, confirming she could hear him but still refusing to talk about Arnie.

Zach wasn't sure what his sister was up to, but he didn't need to over-think it.

They arrived at their destination. "You brought me to a mall?"

"There are seven fine jewelry stores at this mall alone. If you don't find something you like, we'll move on. But we're starting here," Isabelle stated, proud of herself for thinking of this.

"You don't like Amone, though?" Zach questioned.

"Correction. I didn't know Amone. I'm getting to know Amone, and I actually do like her. A lot. So you want to pick out rings or not?" Isabelle asked her brother playfully.

The two visited several jewelry stores before Zach picked out the ring he thought Amone would love. It was elegant and traditional but with just enough detail to make it distinctive. "What do you think?"

"I think if they have it or can create it in white gold or platinum, she'll love it," Isabelle shared. Isabelle tried the ring on to check for size and give it her womanly seal of approval. "This is a seven. I think she'll need a six and a half."

"How would you know that?" Zach asked.

Isabelle smiled and winked at her brother.

"She wears a yellow gold chain so I thought I'd get this to match," Zach said.

"You get an A for observation on that one, Bro. But she bought that chain on vacation because she liked the length. She actually prefers white gold or platinum," Isabelle knowingly shared.

"You have been getting to know her. I'm impressed. And I appreciate it," Zach said as he squeezed his sister's shoulders and kissed the side of her head.

"I like her, Zach. I think she's really good for you," Isabelle said.

"I'm really glad. Me too," he said before turning to the sales person and handing her his credit card. "I've never really been friends with a woman I dated before. Two and a half years is a long time to wait to be with someone. Before it happened, I had pushed the possibility of it completely out of my mind."

"Imagine that," Isabelle said playfully, while the sales person wrapped the ring box and packaged it in a silver bag with a white velvet bow.

"She was worth the wait," he said.

"The best things in life always are."

CHAPTER 8

It had been nearly a week since the young Harriet visited Isabelle, much to Isabelle's disappointment. If she was a figment of her imagination, shouldn't she be able to conjure or summon her at any time? Maybe Harriet was real after all.

On her way to the hospital, Isabelle completely blew through a red light. She didn't slow down or see the light until it was too late. *Oh Lord.* She looked around to see if there was a cop or a camera. *Thank God I didn't hit anyone.* Everything in her world was unraveling at once and it took a toll on everything from her mood to her driving. Even though she seemed to get away with the traffic infraction without incident or consequence, Isabelle started to cry. She wasn't sobbing or making the smallest sound. But big, salty, uncontrollable tears rolled down Isabelle's face one right after another. She wiped her face with her hand several times, only to have her cheeks covered in tears yet again.

In the hospital, Harriet was deteriorating. *I don't want to be running out of time with you too.* Isabelle wasn't always able to visit her aunt during the day, but since she had Grace at night and Arnie was M.I.A., a mid-day visit seemed like the best option. Isabelle hoped it would be enough to coax her aunt to visit her at home once again.

At the ICU, Harriet was still recovering from surgery to

clip her bleeding aneurism. The surgery was considered immediately successful but her long-term outcome was deteriorating. She would likely have a neurological disability, if she did regain consciousness.

There seemed to be an unexplained haze in the air, hanging between Isabelle and the peach-colored walls. The orange and yellow leaves on the trees outside were starting to thin from a prior night of strong winds.

Isabelle sat down and rested her chin on her hand. She took in a deep breath, and exhaled with an exaggerated force before biting her lower lip. She was thinking about what she wanted to say to Harriet. She could feel time running out. *If only life had a gigantic red pause button that we could press when we really needed everything to just stop sometimes.*

Isabelle commenced what turned out to be a softly spoken, almost whispered soliloquy directed at her aging aunt. "I haven't given up on you. I need you to keep fighting. You're one of the toughest old broads I've ever known and I need you to get through this. I need you here, Harriet." Isabelle put her head down. She fought them, but those rolling tears started flowing again, just as when she ran the red light. "You said you would always be here when I needed you, and I'm holding you to that! Because right now, I need you more than ever."

Should I tell Harriet about the divorce papers? What can it hurt? Isabelle had never talked to Harriet about her love life. It was something she considered much too private. But she realized that if there was ever a time, it was now.

"Arnie served me divorce papers today. And while I need you for my own selfish reasons, the truth is, I also want to get to know you for who you are today."

Isabelle paused for the longest time just to breathe. She conjured up the exercise that always helped her relax. *Smell the rose. Blow out the candle. Repeat.* It was simple but it got the job done.

She could feel herself relaxing just a bit as her anxiety inched down. She scooted back into the chair. "The truth is, you weren't an easy person to live with. You weren't an easy person to like. Your continual criticisms affected me. They did. You broke my spirit. I was a little girl and you broke me. Or maybe I was already broken when I came to you and you further broke me," Isabelle's eyes began to tear up again. *Wow! I am really a basket case. I have got to pull it together.* She sniffled some as her speech transitioned into mostly a whimper. The crying was cathartic.

What Isabelle said next had been buried deep inside her for years, and now vocalizing her feelings finally made sense. "What I didn't take the time to realize, I guess, was that you were shattered yourself. Your life was a field of glass. Losing mom, then your parents, then Frank. Just like me, your life was spinning out of control on an orbit you had no map for. And controlling Zach and mostly me, was the only way you knew how to steady yourself and protect us." Isabelle paused again to breathe.

"I think you were probably kind of controlling even before all that happened. I haven't figured that part out yet. But the events that changed my life changed yours too. I lost my parents and you lost your world. We had so much more in common than either of us ever took the time to see." A nurse walked in and interrupted Isabelle talking to Harriet.

"Is everything okay?" she asked.

"As okay as it can be."

The nurse handed Isabelle a warm blanket. "Let me know if I can get you anything else."

"This is nice. Thank you," Isabelle said. A warm blanket was more than a nice touch. It was particularly comforting in the moment. Isabelle needed something warm wrapped around her more than she realized.

The nurse winked at Isabelle as she left. This made Isabelle smile on the inside as it reminded her of something Uncle Frank used to do when he would watch her playing as a child. It brought a familiar warmth Isabelle needed. Isabelle was accustomed to the proverbial flirtatious winks from men, but she had forgotten the way they were sometimes used to create a subtle connection and show support. *This is nice.*

Isabelle wished Harriet had shown a softer, nicer side of herself to her over the years. A part of her was jealous every time she witnessed Harriet's nice side spilled out on strangers and friends. Isabelle picked back up with talking to Harriet, who was still lying motionless in the bed. "You were nicer to your social friends, the people you didn't really care about. You cared what they thought. I used to envy them. I envied how you treated them. But I see now that you couldn't be yourself with them. You couldn't tell them your life was spinning out of control. So you pretended everything was wonderful. But your family – your home – we were your safe harbor to be real."

Isabelle moved ever so slightly in her chair, shifting her gaze from her aunt to the floor, and then back to her aunt. She spoke softly and slowly. The tears had finally stopped at this point. Isabelle had regained some control and composure. "I've been getting to know you. I've been listening. At first, all I wanted was stories about my mom and dad. I wanted to piece my life back together. I wanted to understand why Zach started treating me like you did and why Arnie didn't love me in the end the way he did in the beginning. But the craziest thing happened at some point when I was spending time with the younger version of you who I grew up with – the you that made my life so hard. I started to see you as a person, as someone who experienced pain, fear, self-doubt, hope, and even faith."

Calm came over Isabelle. It was as if she had purged the pain and could finally sit back and make sense of what she was feeling. She was even making sense of her unorthodox visits with Harriet. "And despite your penchant for still correcting every other statement I make, and never just extending the grace to simply let me be me, I started to like you. I always loved you because I knew you loved me in your own way. You made sure Zach and I had a home and as many chances in life as you and Uncle Frank could manage – which were a lot. You were better parents to us than most of my friends who grew up with their natural parents. But love and like are not the same. Love is a commitment. Like is a choice."

She reached out and gently took her aunt's wrinkled hand, something she had never done before. But things had changed. "Over the past month, I have seen you for who you are, experienced your character flaws in living color, and come to realized how enormously important you are in my life. Because commingled with your flaws, I felt your fragile vulnerability. Shining through the cracks in your predominant confidence, I understood for the first time why you always said that no one truly exists inwardly the same way she seems outside herself."

Isabelle leaned in and laid her head on the bed, just to the side of Harriet's heart. There. She said it. All the hurt from all the wounds Isabelle had struggled to hide for most of her life, finally floated to the surface and boldly hung there in the stark uncertainty of the ICU.

Isabelle sat in complete silence except for the beeps from the machines monitoring the patient. Her breathing was so shallow, she almost couldn't hear herself. Her body was numb; she didn't dare try to stand as she wasn't sure she could feel her legs, her feet, or a single thing. Even her thoughts seemed to come to a halt, as she raised her head and torso and stared out the window at nothing. The brightly colored leaves were but a warm blur.

Would everything really end here, like this? She didn't know.

◆ ◆ ◆

At her house, Isabelle sat at the counter in her kitchen, iPad opened to the Pages app. Every time she typed a sentence, she hated it and erased it. She wished she had saved the first sentence. *It's true that the first thing that comes to mind is usually your gut talking to you. If there are any words to listen to, those are the ones.*

She decided to make a list – this time on paper – of all the things she liked about her aunt. Isabelle walked over to the drawer by the phone where she kept a small stack of writing pads. She opened the drawer to grab a pad and pen. She drew invisible circles on the pad as the ink had run dry. She moved her hands around in the drawer looking for a second pen.

The drawer had become a catch-all for rubber bands, a ruler, several screwdrivers, a letter opener, and random other stuff tossed in there over the years. Her face displayed a look of surprise when she ran across an envelope marked 1996. She sighed before turning it over to carefully open the back flap which was tucked into the body of the envelope.

In it were pictures of friends from college. Isabelle didn't remember putting the envelope there. *What a weird place for this.* She thumbed through the pictures, and stopped on a photo of her with Masingho at Multnomah Falls. Her eyes squinted in a warm way, as they often did when good memories flooded her mind. *Was he really the perfect man who slipped away, or have years of being apart only allowed me to remember him that way?*

Isabelle took a deep breath and intentionally stuffed the photos back into the envelope before sliding the envelope under the stack of writing pads. *Harriet. Focus on Harriet. That's what I need to do.*

What did she like about Harriet? She liked the way she

took so much pride in cutting her vegetables for stir-fry with exact precision. She liked it when Harriet would surprise her with random boxes of gluten free snacks and ingredients from the discount basket at the local grocery store. She liked how Harriet would see a jacket or pair of pants that needed hemming, snag them without Isabelle even knowing, and present them to her better than new on her next visit. In her own way, Harriet demonstrated her love for Isabelle, and Isabelle appreciated these efforts.

She was a tough cookie, but she was thoughtful, and generous, when she wanted to be.

Isabelle liked the way Harriet invested in the presentation of things – everything. There were no sloppy dishes or decorations on Harriet's watch. Every package Harriet wrapped looked like it belonged in a professionally staged photo shoot. She liked the way the holidays at Harriet's felt equally homey and luxurious. She liked the way that Harriet grouped the tulip bulbs in the fall so that when they peeked through the dirt in the spring, all the colors matched in a perfect formation. Isabelle smiled as she jotted each one down.

Isabelle realized for the first time that the things she best liked about her aunt co-existed with the same things that drove her absolutely crazy when imposed upon her. Harriet was a slave to precision. And while this dedication led to lovely packages, Harriet didn't reserve her precision for wrapping presents and gardening. She imposed her approach to perfectionism on those closest to her, with Isabelle as her chief target. Isabelle realized that Harriet must have received thousands of compliments on her numerous lovely projects over the years; perhaps she thought that if only she could impose this same characteristic on Isabelle, she too would be appreciated for carrying on such great work.

How strange would it have been, Isabelle wondered, if all this while, Harriet had been trying to help Isabelle obtain the social status associated with the Portland societal ladders she herself had spent decades climbing. Isabelle imagined that Harriet must have had no idea that this wasn't remotely as important to her niece as it was to her. Isabelle had always seen this as controlling, but what if Harriet had intended it to help the woman who had been as close to her own child as she had ever known?

The doorbell rang, so Isabelle left the paper and tablet on the counter to see who was there. It was a delivery service with a bouquet of freshly cut white roses. The vase was adorned by a royal blue bow. Isabelle didn't realize until she returned to the kitchen with the flowers, and saw her aunt standing there, holding the notepad, that she forgot to tip the delivery guy. Isabelle set down the flowers, and bonked herself lightly on the side of her head with her hand. "Happy to see me?" Harriet asked.

"No. Yes, I'm happy to see you, but no, I just realized I forgot to tip the driver," Isabelle said.

"That's why I always keep a short stack of ones in the drawer of the table right next to the door. It's a convenient way to reach over and discreetly pick up a token thank you. Do you have any ones in your purse? I could put a few there for you for next time," Harriet offered as she walked to the drawer by the phone, right where Isabelle had been writing her list.

"It's not like I receive things like this often enough to..." Isabelle got cut off by Harriet before she could finish the sentence.

"This is all you can come up with that you like about me?" Harriet questioned, scanning the list.

Isabelle seemed shocked that Harriet picked up her list without even asking. She put her hands squarely on her hips and as she opened her mouth, before any words escaped, she realized how silly her reaction must seem. *Of course Harriet picked up the list without asking. It's Harriet.*

"I've been putting it off – writing your eulogy. I'm not good at these things. I never know what to say. And the truth is, I don't want to write it." Isabelle said.

"You don't want to honor me?" Harriet asked.

"I don't want to write it because I want you to wake up and fight back. I want to keep getting to know you for who you really are. A vulnerable person who is prickly on the outside and comes unhinged every time someone gets close to figuring out who you are beyond the façade you show the world."

"I don't have a façade." Harriet protested.

"Are you kidding?" Isabelle asked more as a statement. "Gim'me a break, Harriet."

"I don't. I'm exactly what you see."

OMG, she really believes this.

"Listen, I love you, but, there had to be a part of you that resented Zach and me, or resented the fact that you had your tidy world turned upside-down by cruel events completely outside your control when our parents died. You had a life and we changed everything. And then we didn't turn out the way you thought or hoped," Isabelle surmised.

"Oh honey, you've got it so wrong," Harriet's voice lowered.

"So, me sneaking out my bedroom window to meet boys and Zach getting caught with pot didn't disappoint you?" Isabelle asked.

"Well, maybe not all wrong. I was resentful, but not of you."

Harriet picked up the list and carried it with her across the room where she landed on the top of a bar stool. "I resented me."

Isabelle's mouth dropped slightly – but noticeably –

open.

"I finally got what I wanted more than anything on this earth – what I begged for, what I prayed for, what I thought I was entitled to – and it cost me the one person I loved most," Harriet's voice cracked. "And after Joy died, I never felt whole again. I felt selfish and small and out-of-control. So I worked to keep control in whatever small ways I could because I couldn't control the biggest piece of all."

"I don't know what you're saying," Isabelle leaned in.

"Frank and I tried for years but couldn't have children. Joy and Jack got pregnant right away. I thought it was so unfair. I used to nag him to keep trying. Isn't it supposed to be the other way around? Men begging women for sex?" Harriet half laughed at the irony. "Then one day, I got the call. 'The call' that changed everything. Frank and I were parents, instantly. Only the day that happened, Joy left my life and never came back. I envied her so long, and suddenly, everything she had – her most precious belongings were mine. Only I had them without her. I never felt sadness like that. It hung over me and never went away." By this time Harriet was sobbing as tears also streamed down Isabelle's face.

All Isabelle could do was breathe through it. She never knew. She wanted to stand up, walk over and hold Harriet. But she was frozen in place unable to do anything but breathe.

Isabelle only knew Harriet as the grown woman still mourning the loss of her own soul and sacred imaginings, cruelly stolen by the same event that pilfered her own sacrosanct dreams. She never realized the resentments she felt from her aunt all these years were not directed at her, but rather in response to the guilt she faced from raising her sister's children, who she believed only arrived by way of her own covetous, malevolent thoughts. All this time Isabelle knew she wanted and needed more. What she didn't know until this exact moment was that she longed to know Harriet as the only other woman in this world who could walk beside her, take her hand, and brazenly determine that while their pasts were haunted by one tragic event, their futures could be different, brighter, maybe even filled with peace.

Breaking her thoughts, Harriet gestured toward the list. "Well, you left off that I am extremely helpful, give great advice, bring a great deal of wisdom to the table and should always be listened to because I'm always right." Harriet stated matter-of-fact. Isabelle did not want to move on, but she knew that didn't altogether matter, so she went with it. In fact, she completely let go and started laughing hysterically.

"It's a eulogy, Harriet. It's not an obituary and it's not a letter of reference."

Harriet wasn't the least bit phased that Isabelle working on her eulogy meant she expected her to die soon.

"It's a eulogy." Isabelle paused to give her words a moment to sink in. "It's supposed to be about your life," Isabelle clarified. "It's like your hobbies and what you learned and who was important to you – stuff like that. Not that you were always right. Anyone who's going to be there has probably already had you tell them that yourself."

"Is this supposed to be something I like or not?" Harriet asked.

"Well, technically, these things are written after someone passes away to make the family feel good. It's about correcting in death the wrongs that took place in life, or at least smoothing out the things that maybe didn't go so well and accentuating the things that did," Isabelle said.

"I always thought you were a better writer than this," Harriet said shaking her head as she read Isabelle's scribbles. "I think you should scrap this and just tell some of your favorite stories – the nice ones – about me," Harriet directed.

"It's not a finished product. It's notes on a piece of scrap paper. Geez." Isabelle was exhausted, and they hadn't even started on what she wanted to talk about. "What would you like included?" Isabelle asked.

"Leave out all the heavy stuff, the deep lessons. No one wants to hear more heavy stuff at a wake. Make it happy. Start by saying that the loss of Joy and my parents was matched only by the joy of raising Zach and you. I was able to continue to love and see my sister change as you kids grew up. Nothing changes your life more than having kids."

Harriet stopped talking only long enough for Isabelle to interject, "Oh, that's good."

"Raising Zach and you, in a way became her final gift to me, and on some nights, when you snuck out, her revenge on me." Harriet sighed.

"Oh Harriet, I feel so bad for you now," Isabelle said jokingly, intentionally lightening the mood.

"There were a lot of opportunities that came with you two. Travel, school stuff, all your interests. Of course you were also highly challenging,"

"Of course," Isabelle played along.

Harriet paused before adding, "You kids changed my life."

"For the better?" Isabelle asked, smiling.

"Well that's hard to say. You can never know that because you can't live two different lives.

"You're just supposed to say yes to that," Isabelle poked.

Harriet ignored her and almost dipped back into the sentimental. "Raising you and Zach gave me a chance to love Joy even more. Before the accident, I wouldn't have thought that was possible." Harriet choked up just a bit before quickly getting a hold of herself. Isabelle loved this side of her aunt. She never knew Harriet had the depth to love anyone as much as she clearly loved Isabelle's mom.

"Every time I watch you talk about mom, it makes me both miss her and like you so, so, much more. I need you to stay around for a while, Harriet. I need you to recover from this stroke. I feel like I've known you for forty years, and yet it's only recently that I've started truly getting to know you," Isabelle said.

"Well, you've always been absorbed in your own world and I've just done my best to be there for you without ever wanting to necessarily impose," Harriet said. Isabelle could see she and Harriet lived in such contrasting realities. Isabelle tried hard not to laugh. But seeing that Harriet genuinely believed this, she just nodded and said nothing.

It occurred to Isabelle how disparate the divide between the reality we see of ourselves and the experiences of other people. All the while that she saw Harriet so differently than how Harriet saw herself, the same was true on the other side of the looking glass. Isabelle didn't know if it was projection or if they were both blinded to the realities of themselves, but she suspected it was some of both.

Isabelle opened the refrigerator door for a bottle of water. "Would you like one?" she turned to ask Harriet. Just as Harriet had appeared without warning, she was gone.

Isabelle started to chuckle. This whole experience was so weird. *So, so, so weird.*

At least I know what she wants included in her eulogy now.

Isabelle turned back on her iPad and started to write.

CHAPTER 9

The second floor patio at Isabelle's house was perfect for testing Grace's science project. They worked on what Isabelle was sure would be a masterpiece so long as the wind died down enough not to toss Grace's egg back into the siding on the house.

It was in moments like these that Isabelle half wished Arnie was there to help, and just as much wanted to successfully achieve this assignment without him just so she could let him know. "Mom, did you make one of these in school?" Grace asked.

"No, but I remember building a volcano out of clay or mud or something and mixing baking soda and maybe vinegar together to create a lava flow," Isabelle shared.

"Clear lava?" Grace asked.

"It wasn't clear. We added food coloring. Maybe we made it out of flour. I don't know. It was basic kitchen supplies. Science wasn't exactly my thing." Isabelle laughed. "But you know what? We're smart and we have YouTube and I'm certain that someone somewhere has successfully dropped an egg off a roof with a homemade package that prevented it from breaking. We will not have to reinvent the wheel," Isabelle assured her daughter.

"But we have to make it work," Grace said in a tone that reminded Isabelle exactly of Arnie.

"Yes," Isabelle confirmed. "Make it work we will."

After several tries, Isabelle and Grace determined they had created the perfect egg transport system. Grace took popsicle sticks and created a door to keep the egg enclosed in the Styrofoam cup while Isabelle ripped up a second cup to create padding for the egg in the outside cup. They attached this to a paper plate and a balloon.

"Do you think we should decorate it?" Grace asked after hours of creating the gizmo that both were sure would result in a safe landing.

"Yes, but just to be safe, let's make sure it works first," Isabelle suggested.

"Our first one didn't work," Grace reminded her mom.

"Which is good, why?" Isabelle asked, knowing her daughter knew the correct answer.

"Because part of the assignment is writing about our trials and why some didn't work and why the one that worked did," Grace said.

"Exactly. And because in life, things don't always work out. But we learn from them. We make different choices and hopefully we become smarter and stronger along the way, right?"

"I guess," Grace said. She wasn't of an age where philosophical discussions were of much interest to her, but she was aware enough of what was going on with her parents to understand that a lot of extra talking seemed to make her mom happier and cry less. Grace stood up and walked a few feet over to her mom, who was sitting down. The little girl laid her head on Isabelle's shoulder, and looked up tenderly into her eyes. "I love you, mom. Even if this doesn't work."

Isabelle smiled. "I love you too, honey. We're gonna be just fine." Isabelle turned and leaned in to kiss the top of her little girl's head. Isabelle was so relieved that Grace didn't suggest calling Arnie for help.

Arnie was great at figuring stuff like this out, but Isabelle didn't want their daughter believing that only her dad was smart enough to solve a science problem assigned to an eight-year-old.

Isabelle was sure Arnie would have been only too happy to hop right over to help Grace. Tonight, she wanted to figure things out without his constant meddling. She believed that inviting him over would be conceding that they really did need his help.

The big moment had arrived. Isabelle and Grace stood at the top of the second floor patio while Grace dropped the spacecraft-looking gadget containing the egg off the balcony before high-fiving each other. They watched as the egg gently drifted down before turning upside down just before the door flew off and the egg fell out on the grass. They rushed downstairs and outside. Grace discovered the cracked egg on the grass. When Isabelle arrived, she announced the egg's fate, "It's cracked, mom. We need to try again."

"Hmmm," Isabelle said. "Well, I guess it's good we didn't decorate the spacecraft then." It was getting late and Isabelle needed to get her daughter ready for bed.

"Mom, I think you're really smart."

Isabelle was taken aback by Grace's compliment. *What made her suddenly say that?*

"Thank you, honey." Isabelle smiled. And she forced herself to stop there – to put a period at the end of the sentence and just stop talking. Grace was smart and Isabelle recognized that sometimes less really is more. She hated that little voice inside that always needed to be right. *Life with Arnie shouldn't have to be a competition. We both love our little girl.* Isabelle bent down and kissed Grace on the top of her head, and then immediately walked over to the sofa and straightened the cushions and the pillows. *If I have to fix something, it might as well be something that needs fixing.*

More than an hour later, Grace was snuggled in Isabelle's king-sized bed with her when the phone rang, just after ten o'clock. Isabelle was sitting up researching egg transport systems on her iPad. It was Arnie, calling to check on them. He said he was calling to see how Grace was doing, but the truth was he was calling to check on Isabelle, too.

Isabelle told him about the science project and the fact that they already managed to break half a dozen eggs trying to create a solution with just the right cushion and velocity. "How many more trials do you need to document?" he asked.

"Well, we need to document three, and hopefully the next one will be successful," Isabelle said.

"I could stop by tomorrow after work, if that works for you, and help out," Arnie offered.

Isabelle found herself not only agreeing but actually inviting him to come earlier for dinner. *Crap why'd I do that?* Despite how they had grown apart, they would always have the years they spent growing together, and of course their most treasured accomplishment – Grace.

The next day at lunch, when Isabelle stopped by the hospital to look in on Harriet, she took a detour through the hospital gift shop to pick up a card congratulating Zach and Amone on their engagement, along with some bridal magazines.

She wasn't sure when Zach was planning to propose, but she wanted to be prepared when he did. Whether or not Amone was one to thumb through bridal magazines, and whether they would want a destination wedding or something simple at home, Isabelle had no idea. But she wanted to send a clear message of support from the beginning.

"Is this a gift?" the lady at the gift shop counter inquired?

"Yes, my brother is getting married," Isabelle said. "These are for his fiancée." And without being asked, the lady in the gift shop packaged the magazine with a pretty yellow ribbon around the width of it and delicately placed a small bunch of fresh baby's breath into the bow. Isabelle thanked the lady and picked up the pretty package. She smiled. *Just how Aunt Harriet would do it.*

Up in Harriet's room there was no visible change in her aunt's condition. Isabelle sat by her aunt and saw her in a way she never had before, as a vulnerable person just trying to survive like everyone else. In the past, Isabelle always viewed Harriet as strong, difficult and unnecessarily confrontational. But suddenly she saw her more like an older version of herself. The woman who in the past *always had to be right* was like so many others, trying to hide her own feeling of inadequacy and compensating for the mistakes she made and things she held herself responsible for doing wrong.

Isabelle wanted to tell the frail woman in the bed that she understood now, and she loved her despite their differences. Instead, she leaned down and simply said, "You need to fight to get better. To come back. Please get better, Harriet. You don't want to miss Zach's wedding. You don't want to miss watching Grace grow up. You need to fight to live and to get better so you can be a part of it. And I need you to fight to be here for me. I need you Harriet and I love you. Please come back to us."

She reached down, held and then squeezed Harriet's hand. "I know you can do this," she said before turning to walk out.

The truth was that Isabelle didn't know that Harriet would ever come back, and in fact, she had finished her eulogy because she believed that Harriet probably wouldn't. Her prognosis declined each day. But on the off chance Harriet could hear her and understand, Isabelle was determined to be the voice of strength, of hope and of encouragement calling her back from wherever she was.

On the way out of the hospital, Isabelle's phone rang. She didn't recognize the number. She almost dismissed it, but in case it was about Harriet or someone calling from Grace's school, she decided at the last second to answer.

"Isabelle, it's Amone. Zach did it!" she said excitedly.

"Did what?" Isabelle asked, intentionally, as if she had no idea what Amone was referring to.

"I know you know. He proposed. I love the ring and he said I had you to thank for it being platinum because he was going to have it set in yellow gold," Amone confessed.

"Oh wow! That's awesome. And you're welcome. I actually turned him down the first time he asked me to go ring shopping and it was a good thing, because until we met at the falls, I wouldn't have known what type of setting you would have wanted any more than he did."

"I'm so excited. We're so excited. I hope you'll be my matron of honor. We're just going to do something small, maybe on the beach," Amone said.

Wow! Matron of honor? She must have even fewer friends than I do. Isabelle didn't immediately agree to accept this role. It was one thing that they were getting along – even bonding – but they had a ways to go before Isabelle would truly accept her as a sister.

Isabelle side-stepped the invitation by awkwardly changing the subject. "There's a freeze warning tonight. I have several pots I need to pull into the garage when I get home." It was a strange thing to say out of the blue but Isabelle desperately needed a quick turn from the direction the conversation was headed.

While Amone pondered what possibly gave Isabelle the impression that she was a gardener, Isabelle meanwhile replayed the words "matron of honor" in her head. Both women were quiet as they individually tried to figure out the next best thing to say. *I guess Zach didn't mention the divorce papers.*

Now was not the time to bring it up, Isabelle reasoned with herself. This was Amone's moment. Isabelle broke the silence. "Hey, I have something for you. It's small and sort of silly but it's tradition so let me know if you want to meet up for coffee later this week," Isabelle said, looking at the pretty package of magazines she just bought.

"Do you want to know how he proposed?" Amone asked.

"Of course I do, but tell me over coffee. I'm rushing back to the office to finish some things and then trying to leave early. Arnie is coming over tonight to help Grace with her science project and I'm making dinner.

"Perfect. Can I make a bold suggestion?" Amone asked.

"Uh, sure, I guess," Isabelle said.

"Don't forget to take a little extra time to pre-party, for you, not just for him," Amone said in a teasing way. *Pre-party?* Isabelle had no idea what that meant.

"You mean get the crafts set up?" Isabelle asked naively.

"No silly. Pre-party, with yourself," Amone said. There was a long silent pause on Isabelle's end of the phone.

Isabelle's level of discomfort was almost more than she could take. *Could she mean what I think she means?* "Uh," Isabelle started and then paused before adding, "Arnie and I haven't been intimate in a while." Even revealing that was more than Isabelle was necessarily comfortable doing. *Am I a prude or is this oddly inappropriate?*

"Zach told me about the divorce papers."

Should I mention he's dating one of my co-workers?

"Yeah, so, we're just really trying to focus on developing a parenting plan right now."

"Of course. Of course Grace is your priority, but you can change the balance of power here, Izz, if you want," Amone said.

"Balance of power? Thanks, but," Isabelle abruptly stopped mid-sentence.

"Look, the one who cares the least controls the relationship."

"Well, it's pretty obvious that's him," Isabelle said.

"So, what if there was a way to get him to care more? Not to win him back – just to rebalance things. What if you could reignite his interest so that at least you felt like equals again, rather than a victim to him calling all the shots in your relationship?" Until Amone said this, Isabelle hadn't thought of herself as a victim. But she had given him the power in the relationship. And the way he was wielding it about made Isabelle practically feel seasick.

This got her attention. "I'm listening."

"If you come across completely different – alluring, not crazy – you'll get his attention. He'll notice your independence and you'll be like a puzzle he wants to figure out."

Amone does seem to know a lot about men. She got my brother to commit. "Okay, I, uh, don't know exactly what you're talking about," Isabelle said.

Part of her wanted to know and part of her didn't. So against her better judgment, she set her proper inclinations aside to listen to what Amone had to say. She did not commit to taking her advice, only to hearing her out.

Isabelle blushed as Amone shared one of what was undoubtedly her many secrets to seducing men. Isabelle was frankly glad this conversation was via phone and not in person, over coffee, and after Isabelle had just sipped something frothy and hot.

"So he served you with divorce papers. You're not divorced yet," Amone said. "And the great thing about the subtle signs of arousal is that you don't need to say a thing. You'll have a natural glow about you and pheromones that will work on him in primal ways to ensure you don't have to actually do anything different. Think of it as your secret weapon. Then you get to decide how to respond," Amone said, stressing the word "you." Isabelle did like the idea of finally being the one to make some decisions when it came to Arnie rather than just responding to the decisions he made.

"Well, I will give that some thought," Isabelle said, quite embarrassed at Amone's suggestion. She had no plans of giving it any thought. This fell outside of Isabelle's comfort zone. But she humored Amone, in the spirit of building a relationship. "Ok, text me when you're available for coffee. I can't wait to hear about Zach's proposal." Isabelle sighed after she hung up the phone. "Pre-party with myself?" she whispered aloud, embarrassed to even think it, let alone say it, even knowing no one could hear her in the car.

After work, Isabelle pulled chicken breasts out of the freezer to defrost for dinner for Arnie, Grace and herself. She was nervous and wanted to look her best for him, going so far as to curl her hair in the front and freshen up her make-up while Grace worked on her science project in the den.

Arnie arrived early, a bouquet of field flowers in hand for Grace. When he walked through the door, Grace bounced across the house happily screaming, "Daddy, daddy, daddy." He reached down to pick her up and handed her the bouquet of daisies.

"These are for you," he said to his little princess.

Arnie picked up the child and carried Grace to the kitchen where Isabelle was making dinner. "And these are for you," he said with a smile and a peck on the cheek to Isabelle. Isabelle was curious to see what he brought her. He was wearing her favorite blue shirt.

"Sprouted sunflower seeds?" she noted, delighted. "I love these," she said. *They beat divorce papers. What are you making up for now?*

"I know, you're welcome," he said, clearly proud of himself. Isabelle wondered why he hardly did these kinds of small things that showed he cared when they were still together. When they were together, all he cared about were his hobbies and his *big picture plans* to create a better life for them – plans that Isabelle rarely found to hold any promise beyond the pitch.

Why is he being so romantic and thoughtful now? Is he just trying to show me what I'll be missing with him gone? Isabelle wasn't going to fight about this or anything else tonight.

In addition to the salad and chicken, Isabelle had French fry cut potatoes on a baking sheet in the oven. She sprayed them with a bit of olive oil to give them a crunchy texture. French fries were Arnie's weakness, and she knew it. But they were also a favorite request from Grace, so when Arnie displayed his surprise and excitement about Isabelle making French fries, Isabelle casually alluded to the fact that Grace requested them.

After dinner, Arnie and Isabelle cleared the dishes to the sink. Instead of doing them right away, as she normally did, she helped get the materials for the science project laid out.

Isabelle recalled her earlier conversation with Amone. It was totally outside her comfort zone, but watching Arnie with Grace, and thinking about his effort to bring her sprouted sunflower seeds, she decided to go for it. *What can this hurt?* Whether to rebalance the power or just to see if there was any merit to Amone's unusual love potion formula, Isabelle was tired of feeling helpless. *I've already lost my mind. Why not?*

In a nonchalant manner, Isabelle announced she would be right back, and slipped away to her bedroom and locked the door. Afterward, instead of showering, she changed into a matching bra and panties. The lacy red set she last wore on their anniversary. The worst that could happen would be that he would never know.

Isabelle returned as if nothing happened and slid into the chair directly across from Arnie. "Are you ok?" he asked.

"Yes, why?" she wanted to know. *Could he tell already?*

"You're a bit flush and... I don't know. You don't have make-up on but you just look warm and different," he said.

"Mom looks the same to me," Grace said. *Thank you, Grace.*

"I just had to check my iPad really quick," Isabelle lied. "My assistant was going to email me a presentation but she must not have finished it before she left."

"Ok," Arnie said. Isabelle wondered if he could tell she was lying. *Or was Amone right? Could he really sense her phero-mones? Across the table?* Isabelle tried to remember Amone's advice exactly, and not do or say anything different or out of the ordinary. All Isabelle could think of was the possibilities of what might happen with Arnie later. But she had to force her-self to focus on Grace's project. If anything else happened that would be a bonus. "So these are all the materials we can use?" Arnie confirmed.

"Yes, and we already tried a couple methods that didn't work, so now we're looking for that magic design that will bring it home," Isabelle stressed. She knew Arnie was smart and she hoped he would come up with a solution soon so they could test it and she could tuck Grace in bed for the night.

"I think the secret is going to be in how the egg is packaged," Arnie said as he started tearing up the newspaper and creating dozens of tiny crumpled paper balls. He directed Grace to cut up pieces of Styrofoam into smaller shapes than Isabelle and she had done the night before.

Normally, Isabelle would be slightly sabotaging Arnie's first try, to prevent him from gloating over the fact that he was indeed smarter than an eight-year-old. But tonight, she was more interested in watching him succeed quickly, so everything he asked she did without deviating even slightly. He didn't move as quickly as she would have hoped through each step. True to form, Arnie had to stop and consider his plans from every angle. Sometimes Isabelle wished life came with a fast-forward button.

Finally, after putting things together in perfect configuration without tape and glue multiple times, Arnie was ready to help Grace assemble the final product and fly her egg from the second floor balcony. They stuffed the first Styrofoam cup full of crumpled paper balls and Styrofoam pieces, covered the cup with tape and paper, and then nestled that cup into another cup. They then cut a paper plate and wrapped it around both cups, and created a parachute with the newspaper.

On the very first try, the three of them dropped the egg and then ran downstairs to inspect the egg's arrival on the ground. It was a success – a perfect success. The egg wasn't even cracked. *Of course Arnie would create on his first try what Isabelle couldn't do in three.* Normally that would frustrate her. She was competitive by nature. But she was determined to change – to become more accepting.

Tonight was a reminder of how their relationship first started – working together toward a common goal. Isabelle didn't have to be competitive with Arnie when they were working together toward a common goal. The problem was that his new goals did not create a place for her, and as such, she had adapted by developing her own goals and trying to make them bigger, better and more successful than anything he devoted his time to creating in life. And so their efforts, like their ambitions, slowly moved out of alignment and into perpendicular cross-purposes of each other.

"It worked mom, it worked!" Grace shouted with enthusiasm, jumping up and down.

"Yes, honey it did. But for the science fair you'll have to recreate this with your partner, not dad. Do you think you can do that?" Isabelle asked.

"We should probably do some more run-throughs," Grace responded logically.

"Success is ninety-nine percent preparation," Isabelle said, hugging her daughter. Arnie smiled.

Arnie tucked Grace into bed as Isabelle filled the dishwasher and started picking up the kitchen from dinner. After saying goodnight to his little girl, he wandered out to the kitchen and sat on one of the bar stools at the counter. "Need some help?" he asked. Isabelle turned and smiled.

"I've got this," she said sweetly. "Thanks for coming over to help Grace tonight," she said. "It means a lot to me that you follow through every time you promise to help. You're a great dad. Thank you," Isabelle said.

"How have you been?" Arnie asked. Normally this is a question he would ask with trepidation, fearing it might unleash a litany of emotions. But Isabelle seemed so calm and different tonight. It was like a refreshing wave had washed over her and he was sitting in the presence of a new woman.

"I'm good," she said. "Harriett turned a corner today. Zach said her doctor thought it was actually possible she might recover. Can you even believe it?" Isabelle said, almost giddy.

"That's incredible," Arnie said.

"I need to go see her tomorrow morning," Isabelle said.

"I could stop by in the morning to pick up Grace for school, if you want to leave early and stop by the hospital on your way to work," Arnie offered.

"That would be great. Thank you," Isabelle said. Her cheeks were flush and her eyes sparkled. Arnie forgot how radiant she could be.

"Well, I suppose I should go," he said.

"Ok, I'll see you in the morning," she smiled. "Thank you again," Isabelle said.

Arnie walked over to Isabelle to hug her goodbye. He reached his arms around her and only intended to stay a few seconds, but he was unable to let go. He just stood there, hugging her and burying his face in her long hair. She smelled so wonderful, so comforting and familiar.

He pulled away for a moment to look in her soulful eyes that sparkled in the evening light. At the same time, they both leaned in. Arnie was overcome with attraction for the woman he had less than a week ago served with divorce papers. He wondered how this was even possible, but this wasn't the moment to over-think it.

Isabelle enjoyed the spontaneity of the moment. It gave her a whole new respect for Amone's talents for seducing apparently any man, including the one who thought he didn't want her. She felt empowered and this gave her incredible confidence, from which both she and Arnie enjoyed the benefits.

This time, she held the power. How much would she give him tonight? She would decide that as the moments progressed. All she knew at that moment was that kissing him and being touched so affectionately by him made her feel incredibly happy, and so she continued to give him the green light.

Pressed into the counter, Arnie carefully and intentionally unbuttoned her shirt. He immediately recognized the red bra he loved so much. It brought back sensational memories for him. She gently caressed his lips with hers, before pulling back just a little. "I don't want to give you the wrong idea," she said. "I've had a lot of time to think, and while I forgot how much I enjoyed our intimacy, I'm not sure I want to still be married," she said.

Normally, it would have been Arnie saying this. *How have we entirely switched positions here?* But he wasn't in a position to reason with himself or her. He just wanted to be with his wife in the most intimate of ways, and so in the moment, he agreed to anything she said.

"I love you, Isabelle," he said. "It's like you're a different person – the person I first fell in love with, and we can take however much time you need to figure this out," he said.

If only love were enough to make two people compatible.

For the first time in Isabelle's life she knew what it felt like to want sex for the pure pleasure of it and not for the connection it represented. But they had a daughter to think about, and despite her primal yearnings, she had to make a decision in the heat of the moment that was in the best interest of her daughter. "I know," she said. "I want this too. But this could be confusing to Grace."

Arnie didn't want to stop but he was suddenly receiving a very large, almost blinding yellow light from Isabelle. If this had been any other woman, and not the mother of his child, he might have waged a more convincing argument to stay. But he had a much larger goal in mind, or at least to now consider. "You're right. Perhaps we should talk about this when we've had a little less wine." He laughed.

"Fair enough." Isabelle tipped her head to the side sweetly, and invited him to spend the night in the guest room. Arnie had drank more than half the bottle of wine that night while Isabelle carefully monitored her consumption.

"I hope I don't get up to use the bathroom and accidentally forget which bed I'm sleeping in," Arnie teased.

"If it will help, I can lock my door," Isabelle offered. "I don't want to tempt you unfairly or be a tease," Isabelle said. A tease was exactly what Isabelle wanted to be that night. Arnie took her at her word, and he didn't want to push her. A voice in his own head gave him pause about having initiated divorce proceedings. He knew at once he needed to at least consider putting the divorce on hold for a time.

"I know we've been through a lot but I feel like I'm seeing a side of you I haven't seen in a long time, maybe ever. I'd like to maybe explore what seems so new if you're also up for it," he said, leaning in to kiss her on the forehead before turning to leave the room and make his way to the guest room.

Isabelle's jaw dropped. "Wow!" she whispered, half to herself and half aloud. She had never experienced anything like this. It was far more intoxicating than the inch of wine still left in the bottle, which she poured into the sink before tossing the bottle in the recycle bin and turning out the light.

CHAPTER 10

Isabelle awoke early, showered and dressed in a blue suit with white piping trim. She wanted to see Harriet before work, and see firsthand the recovery Zach spoke of via phone. She didn't get a chance to see Arnie before she left, which gave her unexpected relief. She absolutely didn't want to behave awkwardly around him, and she didn't trust herself to remain mysterious "the morning after." *After what? We didn't really do anything. We kissed. Felt each other up a little.* Isabelle smiled. *That was nice. Maybe I need a boyfriend.*

Before heading upstairs to the ICU, Isabelle stopped in for a few minutes to light a candle in the chapel. She sat down to silence her heart and prepare for whatever news was to come. Isabelle was filled with a hope she hadn't felt in quite some time. For the first time in as long as she could remember, she no longer felt like a victim of her circumstances, but rather a woman empowered to face life with her head up and her arms open.

When she walked into the ICU, Harriet's room was empty. *Where's Harriet? Just breathe; everything is okay.* Isabelle immediately made her way to the nurses station where she was given Harriet's new room number, on a general medical floor. Isabelle asked about Harriet's progress, but the nurses cautiously expressed a desire for her doctors to explain her improvements; but Isabelle sensed they were clearly upbeat about the change in her condition.

Isabelle couldn't stop smiling as she walked hurriedly down the hall. Part of it was due to the night before, and part of it was her euphoria over Harriet actually getting better. A few days ago, Harriet's prognosis was grim. It looked like it would be impossible for her to survive and now she had been moved and by all accounts seemed to be doing remarkable. Isabelle thanked the nurses for their news and she rushed to the elevator, more eager than ever to see her aunt.

Harriet was sleeping when Isabelle tip-toed into her room just before seven o'clock. Isabelle couldn't help but notice how Harriet's color had improved. Her aunt looked peaceful and almost healthy without the ventilator. She still had some monitoring wires but the pending sense of death's door was no longer present.

As Isabelle sat down in the leather recliner beside Harriet's bed, the material creaked and Harriet opened her eyes. Isabelle was so delighted her eyes watered as she smiled. Harriet smiled back. "Welcome back," Isabelle said.

Harriet took a deep breath. "Hi," she said.

"You're awake and you look beautiful," Isabelle said.

"Hi," Harriet said again. Isabelle tried not to show any disappointment that Harriet's speech seemed to be limited to only one word. It was tremendous progress. And it was a start toward recovery.

"You don't have to talk. It's wonderful just to have you back," Isabelle said. She wanted to tell Harriet about their conversations the last few weeks. She wondered if Harriet even knew. But that question could wait. This was a new day, and Isabelle was sure it carried new promise.

Harriet smiled and then put her head back and closed her eyes. Isabelle reached out and held her hand. Excitedly, she wanted to tell her about Grace and also about Zach's engagement. She wanted to tell her everything she missed. But before doing that, she stopped to consider that perhaps it was better to not overwhelm her. And she thought Zach might want to share his own good news.

In many ways, Isabelle had changed the last several weeks – and not just for the sake of getting the upper hand with Arnie, although that was certainly a benefit. She had become more aware of her words, her actions, and how her charming, effervescent personality sometimes bubbled up a little too enthusiastically. She determined on her own and for herself that it was okay to be more aware of what she was doing and how her actions triggered those around her. Isabelle was not changing herself intentionally, and certainly not to please others. She was growing in both her presence and her awareness, and in the process, she felt a better sense of control over herself and her own choices.

Isabelle felt happier and less encumbered than she had in a long time, and it was reflected in how she carried herself and even in how she felt about her surroundings. She sat with Harriet a little longer, until her cell phone buzzed reminding her of a meeting at work and a presentation she still needed to complete. "I'll talk to you soon," Isabelle leaned down to whisper just before walking out. On her way out of the hospital she texted her brother the good news of Harriet's improvement and her new room number for the next time he stopped by.

At work, when Isabelle walked by Tina's cubicle, a small part of her wanted to laugh. Her less secure self might have mentioned something, but Isabelle wasn't a woman who had anything to prove. Whatever Arnie had with Isabelle's co-worker was inconsequential to her at this time. She had her own house to get in order and that's what consumed her focus.

Isabelle was working on her presentation when her assistant showed up with a fall bouquet of white mums and bright orange tiger lilies. It had a gold bow and tucked into the greenery was a card that read, "Izz, Thanks for last night. Arnie."

Isabelle removed the card and slipped it into her purse, before setting the flowers on the table on the far side of her office across the room from her desk.

Isabelle closed her door to prevent the normal stream of what she called "the good morning greeters" from stopping by to greet the day fifty different ways and comment on her beautiful flowers. She wouldn't have minded Tina stopping by to notice her flowers, but of course she didn't.

And so when her assistant asked if she wanted an Americano, she graciously and gratefully accepted the time-saving gesture. Isabelle had a lot to accomplish both inside and outside of work and she could only do so by intentionally directing her focus.

◆ ◆ ◆

After work Isabelle texted Amone to see if she was up for coffee or if a glass of wine sounded better.

Isabelle was thrilled that Amone was only too happy to meet at a local tasting room for a glass of wine. Arnie had Grace so Isabelle didn't have to worry about the time. It was remarkable to Isabelle how different Amone was to her once they connected at the falls. Isabelle was looking forward to having Amone as her soon-to-be sister-in-law.

The women made small talk until Isabelle changed the subject to the topic they both wanted to talk about. "So have you set a date?" Isabelle asked.

"We haven't. I wanted to see when you could get away. We decided to do something in Hawaii, although we haven't picked an island," she said. "I thought you might have some suggestions."

"Oahu has the most amenities if you want to do a more

formal affair, but if you're looking for something quaint on the beach, any island will do. Arnie and I honeymooned on Maui. There's a darling little chapel off to the left on the road to Hana," Isabelle said.

"We just want family. Something small and intimate. Any of those suggestions would be great. We'd love to have Grace be our flower girl," Amone said. "Of course there's no ring bearer."

"Who needs a ring bearer? A flower girl and a few witnesses. Someone to officiate. That's all you need," Isabelle said and Amone nodded. "So how did he propose?"

"Well, he knew I didn't want anything in front of people, which was good. I was over at his house and he asked if I wanted him to make me some tea. I thought it was lovely, but he's also never done that before so I thought it was strange," Amone said and both women nodded and laughed. "So he boiled water." Amone paused.

"Go Zach!" Isabelle jumped in.

"Yes. So he boiled water and brought me a box to choose which kind of tea I wanted, and I told him to just pick one. I wasn't even going to open the box. So he was like, 'No, you need to pick the tea you want.' And I was like, 'It doesn't matter. Just pick something for me.' And this went back and forth a couple of times," Amone said.

"Welcome to marriage," Isabelle said.

"Well, if he had ever even made me tea before, this might have made more sense, but by this time it was slightly frustrating. So I was like, 'Bring the stupid box here and I'll pick something,' and he bounced over like a growing puppy. And that moment I just knew something was up," Amone said.

"You get my brother. You get him in a way I don't think anyone else ever has," Isabelle said.

"So I played along and opened the box of tea and instead

of tea, it had a ring box. By this time, Zach was down on one knee and I just looked down at him and smiled. He opened the ring box and asked me to marry him," Amone said.

"And you said yes," Isabelle said.

"No, I said, 'Yes, but only if you still make me some tea." Amone laughed.

Isabelle loved Amone's feisty spirit. "That's awesome." She knew Amone would be good for Zach.

"So he put the ring on my finger and then he brought me some tea. It was very sweet," Amone said nodding and smiling. "I love him, Izz. He was worth the wait."

Listening to Amone made Isabelle believe in love again. Despite their recent efforts, things with Arnie had become so much harder than it felt like it should be. Arnie was great at fixing things and he sent flowers and did the things he thought were women-pleasers. But it never occurred to him to do anything super unique and romantic like bring Isabelle a tea box and have a ring inside. Isabelle was surprised and impressed by this side of her brother she never really imagined existed. *Amone has brought out the best in him. It's amazing,* she thought, *how something so insignificant could mean so much and feel so big and creative.*

"So how are things with you and Arnie?" Amone asked.

"Good, I guess. You know, he makes effort, I make effort. He doesn't bring me tea. But he did send flowers to work after last night," Isabelle said.

"Last night?" Amone asked.

"We kissed. I did that 'thing' you suggested," Isabelle said. "It was weird but it seemed to work."

"So? Now what?" Amone asked.

"I should ask you that. Now what?"

"Well, don't call him. Don't text him. Make him show up and earn your time and attention. Men only appreciate what they work for," Amone said.

Isabelle smiled and shook her head. "We've been married more than ten years. When does the chase end?"

"It shouldn't end. Do you ever think about how many times you made dinner, changed your sheets or decorated for a holiday?"

"Is that a rhetorical question?"

"No. We all do the same things over again because they need to be done and we want the outcome they produce. We want to be full, to have a clean home, to feel rested to celebrate another holiday. Why wouldn't you put the same effort into your marriage? How do you expect it to thrive if you're actively creating an environment for it to thrive?" Amone asked.

"I never thought of it that way. I guess I thought that with enough years of marriage it should just continue to roll along," Isabelle said, her voice trailing off.

"No wonder you're struggling. You can have your own life – your own interests – in fact, you should! But you also need to remind him why he picked you. Look cute. Smell good. And be nice. But maybe not too nice. You have to be willing to walk away from anyone who takes you for granted – and that goes for any relationship, except your child," Amone advised.

"Should I sleep with him?" Isabelle asked.

"If there's even a little part of you that wants to work things out, no. But if you just have an itch that needs scratching and you're both in the mood, I say why not?" Amone suggested. "You'll know," she said nodding. "Trust your gut."

"Well thanks for the advice," Isabelle said.

"Thanks for the wine," Amone said. "Oh, I'm meeting Zach for dinner. I need to run. Call me," Amone said as both women slid on their coats and grabbed their purses to head out.

A couple days later, while waiting at home for Arnie to drop off Grace, Isabelle picked up the notebook on which she had jotted down key points for Harriet's eulogy. In one motion, she set the glass of wine in her left hand down as she reached over and picked up her iPad in her right hand. With her left hand now free, transferred the tablet to her left hand and navigated to her documents with her right forefinger.

There it was. Finished. The eulogy she resisted writing, and for all she knew had launched this pattern of unorthodox visits from her aunt.

She started to read it over, half wondering if she should just throw it out all together, or keep it for some point in the future. Just as Isabelle thought of her dear aunt making what doctors described as a miraculous recovery, Harriet showed up. Isabelle's heart sank. *Does this mean your rally won't last?*

"Oh, you're back," Isabelle said, disappointed.

"Well don't sound so excited about it," Harriet said.

"No," Isabelle paused. "It's not that I'm not excited to see you. But you were getting better, and I thought maybe you'd be coming home soon – really coming home soon – as yourself, today. Now I'm thinking maybe not," Isabelle said reluctantly.

"I'm home when I'm with you. And I'll be with you as long as you want me to be," Harriet said. "You decide who you invite into every part of your life, Isabelle. Just as I get to decide who I invite into my life," the aunt, who still appeared very close to Isabelle's age said to the niece that was more like a daughter to her. "When we love someone, we hold them in our hearts. They are with us no matter where we are and no matter the circumstances, situation or environment. If I can give you anything, that's what I most want to leave you with to know – not just say or agree to – but really know with every part of you."

Isabelle reached her right hand to her face and massaged her sinus passages on her face. She did it subconsciously, in response to years of battling allergies and using this technique when she felt pressure building. She inhaled and exhaled slowly. "I was just reading over your eulogy. I'm trying to decide if I should finalize it or wait until I hear something more concrete," Isabelle said.

"Do you want to read it to me?" Harriet asked. "I'm always happy to give you my opinion," the aunt said matter-of-fact, which made Isabelle laugh.

"Wouldn't that be weird?" Isabelle asked.

"Don't make me beg you. Read it to me," Harriet insisted.

"Okay," Isabelle began.

"We spend half a lifetime preparing to lose certain, special people in our lives. As bitter as we know that day will be, and as much as we work to ensure it doesn't arrive a moment before it must, we all understand the cycle of life.

"We're born. We live. We love. We change – hopefully for the better. We die. And time ticks on. Just as great love is expected as we reach our coming of age, great loss is inevitable as we inch ever closer to middle age. And so we start the dialogue with ourselves early. We prepare ourselves. We embrace the moments we have with those we love, and we plan for that fateful day when we will wake up without them here. It's like snow coming to the Cascades in fall or winter. We cannot predict the day in advance, but we know the time to expect the changing of the seasons. And yet, even when we have time to prepare, somehow it's never enough."

"Isn't this supposed to be about me?" Harriet asked.

"It is about you. That's just my introduction," Isabelle

clarified.

"I think you just need to start with the part about me," Harriet directed.

Isabelle smiled, then laughed, and began again. "Harriet Zelner was born May 16, 1945 in Ellensburg, Washington to Mae and James Barth. She was their first daughter and older sister to Joy Barth-Gordon, my mom. They lived on a farm with apples, cherries and other fruit.

"She was a precocious child who discovered a magic key at a very young age that would protect her against the influence of others and ultimately frame her life. No matter what anyone said or thought, Harriet had captured the confidence to believe she always knew best and she was always right."

Harriet interrupted, "You need to reword that. It makes me sound stubborn and bossy."

"Actually, that part was a joke to see if you were listening," Isabelle said.

"Well, just reword it. We don't want to give anyone the wrong impression," Harriet decreed.

Isabelle snickered as she continued the eulogy. "When Harriet was 22, she met and married Frank Zelner, in a traditional church wedding on June 20, 1967. When Frank's job relocated him to Portland, this one-time country girl followed her love and created a whole new life for herself. She immersed herself in the Portland social scene, investing her time, talents and money in many of Portland's cultural icons. She had many friends, to whom she was gracious, hospitable and generous. She was a wonderful aunt to my brother Zach and me.

"I was five years old the first time Aunt Harriet took me shopping at the Clackamus Town Center. It was the first mall I remember visiting, and it was filled with what seemed like thousands of stores. I felt like a princess, and I'm sure it's the combination of that day and Aunt Harriet who I have to blame for commencing my love affair with shopping and carrying armfuls of stylish and brightly-colored bags down long corridors of shops. From the time we were young, Aunt Harriet spoiled Zach and me like we were her own children."

Isabelle's tone changed as she continued. "When Zach was ten and I was eight, the unthinkable happened and our worlds changed forever. Our parents were killed in a car accident. Uncle Frank and Aunt Harriet immediately stepped up to welcome us into their forever home. It was only recently that I realized that it wasn't just Zach and my hopes and dreams that shattered that day. Losing mom was the single hardest thing Aunt Harriet faced her whole life. It changed her in ways I didn't realize for more than thirty years.

"Uncle Frank and Aunt Harriet were more than an uncle and aunt to Zach and me. Uncle Frank always had the easy role. He was the good cop – and a great buddy. He was fun, from a kid's view of the world. He played with us and let us taste his beer on camping trips when we went fishing."

"Oh Frank. I knew he did that, even though he said he never did," Harriet exclaimed.

"Aunt Harriet was the glue that held the family together. Glue is sticky and stubborn. It holds things in place – which can be good and essential and necessary. It is impossible to raise a family without the glue. As kids, it's easier to appreciate the fun adult; but as an adult, I've really come to appreciate the glue that held us together." Harriet stopped interrupting and grew uncharacteristically quiet.

"Harriet loved to supervise and she always had advice to share, even about things she didn't know much about. It used to drive me crazy until one day not long ago when I asked her why she did that. She said that her lifetime of experience was the culmination of everything she learned – and that in sharing her advice – mostly unsolicited – it was her way of sharing with those she loved, or felt she could help, the benefit of knowledge she picked up along life's journey. It was in that conversation that I also learned that sometimes understanding where someone else is coming from may not make everything easy, but at least it puts things in perspective." Without missing a beat, Isabelle reached up and quickly dabbed away one tiny tear that had escaped the outer rim of her right eye.

"Harriet loved all things living. She loved plants and animals. She once admitted to me that she didn't start out as much of a gardener. It was something she picked up to remember her sister and our mom, Joy. That was hard for me to believe, because as long as I knew Harriet, she was the best gardener I could ever imagine. She could make just about anything grow, including numerous half-dead houseplants I dropped off over the years. She had a money tree that was over seven feet tall. We're donating that to the arboretum, by the way, as God knows I wouldn't be able to keep it alive and a tree that beautiful really deserves to be cared for by someone who knows how.

"Uncle Frank was not a pet person and was not keen on Zach and me getting a dog. Harriet convinced him it would be a good opportunity for us to learn responsibility. Soon, there were five of us on every camping trip and other adventures by car. Frank, Harriet, Zach, me and Diesel. Like most dogs, he got that name by default. I don't remember what we initially called him, but as a puppy, one time he got into a can of diesel up at grandpa's farm in Ellensburg. Zach asked what that smell was and without missing a beat, grandma answered "diesel." After that we changed his name.

"Three years later we had a dog, two cats and a lizard. Harriet didn't know this, but she and Frank taught me that when you open your home and your heart to others, you sometimes get more than you bargained for. But the love they give you back more than compensates for the love and effort you extend to them. This is true for animals and humans I've found." Isabelle paused to lick her bottom lip and smile.

"Harriet always liked to be right – even when she was wrong there was never a point in arguing with her because she was not one to concede a debate. As a teenager, and even as a young adult, this contributed to more than one clash of personalities. She saw everything black and white, in a world that was increasingly sketched with shades of gray and color. One time I confronted Harriet about this frustrating style of thinking she had, and while she never actually said this, Harriet conveyed that she always tried her best to do what she thought was right and she believed in what she felt was right. After that, whenever I overheard her telling anyone she was right, including telling me she was right, I silently inserted the words 'I try to do what's right.' Instead of it bothering me so much, in her own way, she inspired me. Because really, well-placed conviction is an admirable characteristic, and one we just don't see much of anymore. Shouldn't we all try to do, feel and say the things we believe to be right and bring about good?

"In her later years, Harriet taught me how to better appreciate the ones we love. She reflected on her own love story with Frank in advising me to think about the effect our words and actions have on others. For someone thrust into motherhood out of grief, she really was a very committed and strong role model for a young girl, and later a middle-aged woman still floundering about in life. Sometimes leading with hugs and love, and other times with the warning of a reprimand, she helped me discover my wings, try them out, and use them to both fly out into the world, and just as importantly, safely return back home. She always followed, 'I warned you about this,' with tenderness and open arms.

"Aunt Harriet, despite all the challenges we have faced together over the years – the agreements and the disagreements – the memories you want to remember and those pesky things we all do that everyone hopes others will forgive and forget –

there are three things I want you to always know. I love you, I thank you, and I will forever miss your feisty counsel, always followed by tenderness and open arms. I have so immensely cherished getting to know you, really know you, the last piece of time we have shared.

"I hope to be even half the sister to Zach that you were to Joy. You carried mom's legacy, mom's grace and mom's precious love for her children forward when you created a home and a life for us. She would have been so very proud of you, and immensely grateful for your selfless gift of sacrifice you gave the babies she was unable to raise. And if you ever decide to show up in my kitchen unannounced in the future, my home is your home and always will be, just as you once made your home mine. Yes, for this and everything else, thank you. I love you. And as it turns out, I also really like you, and I will miss you as long as I draw breath."

Isabelle and Harriet were both emotional by the time she finished the somewhat-lengthy and heartfelt ode to her aunt. Without saying a word, Harriet walked over and took the grown child in her arms. "What do you think? Do you like it?" Isabelle asked.

"Oh honey, everyone should feel this appreciated at least once in her life. But now I need you to do something very important for me," Harriet said.

"What's that?" Isabelle asked, even more tears welling up. Isabelle realized she wasn't at all ready to say goodbye to Harriet, and she feared that is what she was about to ask.

"I need you to keep this in a safe and special place, to share when it's truly appropriate," Harriet said.

"What do you mean?" Isabelle asked.

"I'm not ready to go yet. I'm getting stronger every day, and you, my child, have a beautiful, smart, amazing, precious little girl I want to watch grow up. I put my time in as a surrogate parent, and I'm darn well not giving up the chance to be Yia Yia to Grace," Harriet said, expressing slight humor.

"You're getting better?" Isabelle asked, confused.

"Every day," Harriet confirmed. "I can feel it."

"So why did I spend so much time working on this stupid thing?" Isabelle asked, wiping her tears, sniffling and smiling.

"Everything in life is part of the process, whether we know it at the time or not," Harriet said. "Each moment, no matter how seemingly inconsequential, gets us to the next."

Just then the front door opened. It was Grace and Arnie getting home. Isabelle was happy to see them both, even though she still had no idea where things would go with the man she still loved, although not necessarily in the same way she once did. She had changed. Maybe he had too. At the very least it was something Isabelle had to investigate.

"How was your day?" Isabelle asked Grace.

"Awesome. We did a run through on the egg drop at school for the science fair," she said. "Have you been crying?" Grace asked.

"Yes. I just read a sad story. But I'm okay now that you're home telling me about your day. How did your project go?" Isabelle redirected the conversation.

"It worked the first two times but not the third time. So we came in second," Grace explained.

"But the science fair is tomorrow, I thought?" Isabelle questioned.

"If the run-throughs today had been the finale, her partner and she would have come in second. The science fair is tomorrow. We thought we'd run through everything again tonight," Arnie announced.

"Sure," Isabelle said. This wasn't what she had planned,

but she was willing to go with it. Isabelle thought she had the night to be home alone catching up on the news or doing something else she enjoyed. "Do you guys want to get started while I make dinner?" Isabelle asked.

"We can do that," Arnie said. Isabelle would have liked it if Arnie would have set up place-settings on the bar or even offered to help, but he didn't, so she took care of it while the turkey burgers were cooking on the barbecue. As far as he had come in certain areas, there were others that, after more than a decade of Isabelle trying to train him, still didn't come natural. But whereas Isabelle would have let it rile her in the past, today she was in a better position to let some of these things go for her own peace of mind.

"Thank you for the flowers," she told Arnie. "They were perfect." She winked at him.

It was obvious by the look of satisfaction on his face that he needed to hear this. As Arnie turned to help Grace, Isabelle's focus also shifted. To Harriet. She had this nagging feeling of non-closure. *Is this it? Will I see you again Harriet? If you do get better, will you have any recollection of our visits?* Isabelle scratched an itch on her neck before lifting the grill lid to turn the burgers. She had mostly come to terms with her inability to distinguish between reality and the aberration that had become uncharacteristically real over the past several weeks.

Just like before, the three of them made run-throughs. And then also like before, Isabelle excused herself to check her iPad, once again locking the bedroom door in case Arnie came exploring the house prematurely. But when she was dressed and ready to rejoin her family, Isabelle felt a noticeable hesitation. She thought about how misleading Arnie had become, and she no longer cared about having sex with him, whether or not she could. She was thankful he was such a great dad to Grace, but that fact alone did not make him a great partner for her. If Grace were not in the picture, who Arnie had become no longer met the standards she wanted for her life. She didn't judge him, but she also didn't want to get intimate with him, not tonight anyway.

It was a startling realization for her. She recognized now that sometimes small things change people in big ways. She had changed. What she wanted for her life and how she valued herself had changed. Isabelle came to the place where she could delineate between what she could have and what she would settle for both from herself and others.

Isabelle entered the kitchen with a confidence she had not owned for a very long time. When Arnie looked up at her, he sensed something was different, but he couldn't put his finger on it. Isabelle took a seat at the bar next to Grace, as she often would. But this was no ordinary evening. An axis had shifted. She was different, and it scared him, because for the first time he sensed he had lost all control of her.

Isabelle noticed how smitten Arnie had become with her. Why couldn't he have shown a fraction of this interest when she still wanted him to, she wondered. Poor Arnie, she thought – always searching for what he truly couldn't have, and never genuinely wanting the cornucopia of love and affection set before him while it was still his to be had. She didn't want to have to turn him down. In fact, she hoped he would cycle through his interest before she had to send him home.

When it was time for Grace to go to bed, Isabelle volunteered. Her plan was to fall asleep next to her child, expecting at some point Arnie would simply get tired of waiting and go home. But he jumped in, and so Isabelle quickly altered her plans as well. "Thank you so much for coming over to help us figure this out," she told him, half hugging him, rubbing her flat palm up and down his back as she would to comfort any friend.

"Don't go anywhere. I'll be right back out," he said, winking playfully.

"Oh Arnie, I'm so tired. I'm just going to turn in. Would you mind locking the front door as you leave?" Isabelle asked.

"Are you sure?" Arnie asked, obviously surprised. She was well aware that he was expecting a repeat of the night they kissed, only ending in the bedroom they once shared. And to be honest, less than an hour ago, so did she.

"Yes, I'm sorry. I'm just exhausted," Isabelle said. "But I'll see you tomorrow at the science fair," she said smiling.

"Okay. I'll pick up wine for afterward," he said. "I'm thinking positive that we'll have a blue ribbon to celebrate."

"That sounds great. Thanks. Good night, Grace. I love you. Good night, Arnie," Isabelle said before turning toward her bedroom. Arnie watched her walk away, half expecting her to turn back and smile or look his direction. He was confused at what transpired. How had she changed so much in such a short time, he wanted to ask, but didn't for fear he might hear an answer he didn't want verbalized.

For the first time in a long time, Isabelle went to sleep almost immediately after her head touched the pillow. She finally found the sense of peace she had been seeking. She didn't lock the door, and she didn't hear Arnie turn the handle and open the door to her bedroom to check on her. He watched her sleep for a minute or so, and then quietly and gently turned the handle and shut the bedroom door before, almost by habit, checking all the other doors and then leaving out the garage.

As he watched the garage door close from the driveway, he felt a raw sense of regret for not feeling this connection to his wife while their marriage could still be saved. He watched the garage door close and drove away down the same street that had taken him home for the last several years. "We will fix this tomorrow. I will fix this," he voiced aloud, despite that there was no one else in the car to hear him. Saying it aloud made it real. He was determined to win back her heart one more time.

CHAPTER 11

I sabelle was at her desk when the call she hoped and even prayed for came in. It was Harriet's nurse calling to say that doctors were discharging Harriet. She had not made a full recovery but she had come far enough to meet Medicare's requirements to go home with home health care checking in. Isabelle was hesitant to believe the news at first, and even asked if Harriet should go to an outpatient rehab center to get stronger. But the doctors felt she was ready to go home and the discharge orders were being processed.

What a rollercoaster the last several weeks have been. This is what Isabelle wanted – for Harriet to recover and be able to go home. She just didn't think it would be so soon – the night of the science fair. She thought about how she could be in two places at once. *Like Harriet!* She half laughed to herself. Isabelle wanted to feel giddy but without talking to the doctors or seeing Harriet in person it just seemed too good to be true.

Isabelle powered through her projects. It would mean leaving early yet again, and she wasn't sure just how much flexibility her boss would continue to give her. Salvador had been extremely understanding, as someone who lost his own mom a year before. Isabelle didn't want to press her luck. She knew every piece of elastic only had so far to extend. But she was in the home stretch now, she concluded; Harriet would be home soon and she could return to her familiar life and schedule. Just another week and everything would be back to normal.

When Isabelle entered Harriet's hospital room, she was surprised to see her aunt dressed and waiting for her in a wheelchair. "Wow, they're not going to let any grass grow under you," Isabelle said.

"It's been a busy morning," Harriet said slowly and with intention for each word. Isabelle could sense there would be a long recovery following the stroke, but she was happy Harriet had recovered enough to go home. "Is Zach coming?" Harriet asked.

"Oh no. He's taking off early to go to Grace's science fair tonight. I'm so sorry that I can't be home with you tonight but I can't miss the science fair," Isabelle said with sincere regret. "Of course I would have been at home with you on your first night. It just happened suddenly and tonight of all nights." Isabelle cringed a little inside imaging how this must sound. She didn't mean her aunt was a burden, but she also couldn't let her daughter down.

"I want to go," Harriet said.

"We will. We need to wait for the discharge from the doctor and then I'll take you home," Isabelle said.

"To the science fair," Harriet said slowly.

"You want to go to the science fair?" Isabelle asked. "I don't know if that's a good idea."

"Ask doctor," Harriet persisted. Isabelle had to chuckle a little. Despite how far Harriet and she had come the last few weeks in their own world together, Harriet was still the stubborn and determined lady she always knew.

"Okay. We'll see what he says," Isabelle conceded. There was no point arguing without more information.

As it turned out, the hospitalist cleared Harriet to attend the science fair when he discharged her, and only asked that she use the wheelchair or walker until her balance and strength returned. She would have no problem walking on her own again following physical therapy, which Isabelle was relieved to hear. *Perhaps it's time to start thinking about selling the house and moving Harriet to senior living.* Isabelle had a habit of getting ahead of herself and thinking six steps beyond whatever was currently going on.

"I'm glad you're coming home," Isabelle told Harriet during the car ride. "We'll get you settled and give you a chance to rest before we head out to the science fair this afternoon," Isabelle said. The look on Harriet's face showed her approval.

Talking to the apparition of Harriet had become so easy. Now with her aunt physically sitting in the car beside her, Isabelle was rendered speechless. *There should be so much to say, where do I begin? Do I ask her now about her phantom visits? Do I ever mention the eulogy? What do I do with it?*

The car ride back to Harriet's was mostly silent. It took a medical crisis to silence her aunt. Isabelle almost missed the chatty version who cycled through ten topics in twelve minutes. *Maybe someday she will be somewhere in the middle.*

"Are you tired?" Isabelle asked.

"No. I am happy to see the world through more than a dingy, streaked window." This sentence took Harriet nearly two minutes to get out because she had long pauses between each word. When Isabelle started to speak to help finish her sentence, Harriet moved her left hand to swat at Isabelle. "I can speak," she started, again with long pauses between each word. "Don't speak for me."

In any other situation, Isabelle would have laughed. *This is so Harriet. Still in control.* But part of becoming more accepting of others meant that Isabelle also started imagining herself in the mind of the other person. *This must be so frustrating for her.* At a red light, Isabelle took Harriet's hand, the hand that had just swatted at her, and turned to face her. "I love you. I'm glad you're getting better."

Harriet smiled and started to tear just a little. "Me too."

Walking into the school gym where the science fair was held was like walking into a party. *The PTA has really outdone themselves.* It was the perfect celebratory homecoming for Harriet. Isabelle had once considered joining the parent teacher association. It was a group she supported, but work and priorities had not afforded her the time to make such a commitment. Perhaps she would get herself and Harriet more involved in this as Harriet got stronger. *Harriet will need something to occupy her time.*

Brightly colored streamers and garden lights were strung from one side of the gym to the other. Various parts of the gym were sectioned off, dividing the areas into color blocks devoted to second graders, third graders, fourth graders and fifth graders. Each area was distinguished by a different theme and different colored streamers. Grace was in third grade and her color was red. Red was Isabelle's favorite color. Each area also had its own judge who patrolled the area to ensure no cheating.

Third grade competitors were divided into pairs and given a time limit. They had one shot to prove themselves. Zach and Amone were already there when Isabelle wheeled in Harriet. When Grace saw Harriet she left her post and ran across the area yelling "Yia Yia, Yia Yia, you're better!" which put an enormous smile on the older lady's face.

The judge stepped over to the family and informed Grace that if she didn't return to her project post she would be disqualified. "I just picked her up from the hospital today. Grace is just happy to see her," Isabelle told the judge.

The judge wrinkled her nose in the form of a scowl before saying, "We can't give one child an advantage over any other team. It wouldn't be fair."

"Harriet had a stroke. She can barely talk. We won't violate the rules. I promise," Isabelle said.

The judge clearly was proud of herself for not relenting, nodding appropriately. "You wouldn't want another child receiving an unfair advantage, and I have to be fair," the judge said.

When the science fair judge walked away, Zach leaned into Amone and Isabelle and sarcastically added, "Good thing she doesn't take herself too seriously."

"Hey, where is Arnie?" Isabelle asked.

"I don't know. He was here earlier," Zach said, glancing around the room for him. Isabelle left Harriet, in a wheelchair, with Zach to wander around looking at the displays.

"I'd offer to buy you a glass of wine but they're only serving tea, lemonade and water, I'm afraid," Amone said, walking up behind Isabelle.

"Too bad. I'd take the wine," Isabelle said laughing, reaching out to accept a clear plastic cup of iced tea and lemonade.

"So," Amone said, and then paused, "How are things going with Arnie?"

"I don't know," Isabelle said.

Amone looked at her and then her face changed. "Oh, you really don't know. What did he do now?" Amone asked.

"Nothing. I mean, he's fine," Isabelle said and then stopped for a few seconds. "He's a great dad, and a decent man. And if I bit my lip enough and changed enough things about me and my preferences, I could probably make it work. But how long do I want to be someone I'm not to attract someone I don't enjoy being with anymore, and furthermore, don't completely trust?"

"Well that's something only you can know," Amone said.

"People change. He's changed. I've changed," Isabelle started. "I thought maybe we changed separately in ways that made sense together; but even though we're both making more effort than either of us has in a really long time, we're still very different."

"He feels this way too?" Amone asked.

"I don't know what he feels," Isabelle said. "I've spent our entire marriage thinking about what he wants. He likes camping. I go along. He likes car shows. I go along. Whenever he's home the television is on. Why can't he just read a book or do something quiet sometimes? Why can't he sit and talk to me in the kitchen while I make dinner for the family? It's like I'm his maid. And he doesn't even say thank you or show appreciation. He critiques everything I prepare like I'm opening a new restaurant and he's a newspaper critic. 'Gee Izz, did you forget to salt this?' Would it hurt him to dice up the onions or peel and core the apples? Would it really hurt him to help me?" Isabelle didn't realize she had so much built up inside.

Isabelle expected Amone to say something, anything, but she didn't. "When we were together, I kept thinking that if I just put him first long enough, he'd want to do the same for me. But it never happened. He lives in his Peter Pan world of dreams and hobbies. He's still the guy who thinks sex will save a relationship – or save whatever it is he thinks we have," she said.

"Have you talked to him about this?" Amone asked.

"I've tried," Isabelle said, and then paused before continuing. "Either I'm doing what he wants and he's fun and I don't want to spoil it. Or I push back and he gets quiet and leaves the room."

"It sounds like there's very little scope for mutual satisfaction," Amone said.

"You have no idea how much I wish I could make it work. I love him. He drives me bat-poop crazy, but he's a good man, a great father, and I will probably always love him."

152

"Sometimes love is not enough. Sometimes compromise is not enough, especially when one person feels like they are doing the lion's share of giving and stretching," Amone said. "Have you had this conversation with him?"

"I don't know that it would do any good. I need someone I can depend on. He's a great dad to Grace but after the way he tricked me into meeting him for pizza and making me sign for divorce papers – I just don't know if I can bring my guard down enough to trust him. And did I tell you he's dating one of my co-workers?" Isabelle asked, not expecting an answer but getting one. "That was such a special surprise."

"No way. He's dating someone else? Someone you know?" Amone asked, upset in a way someone might be if they were working secretly to help two people get together only to realize one of those people wasn't giving them the whole or true story.

"She texted him a picture of me dancing with some random guy at a pub and then added a snide remark about him not needing to worry about me, that I was fine and had moved on, which was complete bullshit," Isabelle informed. "Oh, and this is after she came to my office and asked if I had a brother named Arnie and told me he kissed her."

I never used to swear. Arnie has driven me to drink and swear.

"No way."

It's not Arnie. I chose this.

"Look, I was blind-sided and devastated by the divorce papers. I was. And I appreciate your 'unconventional' tips on se-ducing him back. They actually made me feel attractive again, even to him, that he wanted more," Isabelle said sincerely. "But beyond the challenge of getting him back, I have to ask myself if I really want him back in my life romantically. And I haven't come to a decision." Isabelle sounded sad because she was sad – for Arnie. She felt betrayed by the one person she never dreamed would betray her. Oddly enough, that didn't make her angry at him. But it gave her the strength to begin asking herself what she wanted and what she was willing to sacrifice – or not.

"Well, the night is young," Amone said, just as Arnie came up behind the women.

"The night is young? Are you feisty creatures thinking about sneaking out for a nightcap?" Arnie asked, in jest.

"Hey Arnie. I'm going to find Zach," Amone said before leaning in to peck Isabelle on the cheek. "Good luck."

"Good luck?" Arnie asked. "Did I interrupt girl talk?"

"Good luck on Grace winning her division," Isabelle bluffed. Arnie nodded but had disappointment written on his face. Isabelle could tell he wanted "good luck" to be about him.

"Hey, I have something for you," Arnie teased, pulling a flask out of his pocket.

"The last time you said that you handed me divorce papers," Isabelle said in an uncharacteristically passive-aggressive way. Arnie got uncomfortably silent.

"Uh, vodka. I was going to say I had had a little fire water to turn your Arnold Palmer into a John Daly," Arnie said.

"Well, that I'll take," Isabelle smiled and said playfully back. "As long as it doesn't require a pen," she added, trying to be funny. He wasn't laughing and things were going south so she quickly followed up with, "I hope you don't think this sampler size vodka gets you out of bringing wine to celebrate if Grace wins the blue ribbon tonight."

Finally, she made him smile. She wasn't sure if she wanted to celebrate with him later or not, but if there was anything she had learned from Amone, it was to keep her options open.

Like her brother, Arnie could be moody sometimes and there was no easy way to bring him back if he slipped too far in that direction. *I guess we're not all that different.* Isabelle half chuckled to herself but didn't share what she was laughing about with Arnie.

"It's nice to hear you're thinking about celebrating," Arnie said.

"Well, I'd like to think our hours of hard work designing and creating an egg parachute will pay off." Isabelle winked.

Arnie didn't know what to make of this familiar-looking woman to whom he was technically still married. Isabelle didn't play games like this normally. He didn't recognize this person who was back and forth, one minute inviting and the next shutting him out. If there wasn't so much at stake he would have enjoyed the chase. But he sensed that for the first time, maybe she wasn't all in. He sensed that maybe he didn't have this in the bag after all. He sensed that the smallest misstep could blow the whole thing apart, and he couldn't risk that. He was, after all, determined to win back her heart.

The master of ceremonies took the stage. "It is now time for the judging to begin," he announced in a serious and formal tone. Isabelle and Arnie joined Harriet, Zach and Amone. They started with the second graders.

The science fair was lasting longer than Isabelle planned, and she was unsettled about Harriet being out so late and not having dinner or her medications. Fortunately, the school offered a chili cook-off hosted by the PTA. So instead of being served an actual bowl of chili, each person was served a plate filled with eight paper nut cups, each filled with a tablespoon of a different parent's chili. With her food allergies, this did not seem like a good idea. But to support the PTA, she bought a round for the whole family and handed her portion over to Arnie and Zach.

Isabelle frequently thought about inappropriate things that amused her. Most of these she kept to herself. *If only* she had shared this silly side of herself with Arnie, they could have appreciated the charm of her weirdness together. He would have loved this. But she never let him into this part of herself.

So after passing out the chili to her family, she walked to the side of the gym so she could amuse herself with her own jokes about a gym filled with gassy guests. Isabelle sang a familiar tune in her head. *Bean, beans the magical fruit. The more you eat the more you toot. The more you toot the better you feel. So eat your beans with every meal. Awe, what I don't do for my daughter.*

Noticing her off by herself, Arnie came over to stand beside her. He placed his palm in the small of her back. "What do you say we rip up the papers for now?" he leaned in and whispered.

"What?" she asked.

"Look, things may not work out for us long-term," he said. "But what if we just rip them up for now or decide to not file them to give us some time to figure out if that's what we really want?"

Isabelle never imagined Arnie would make this offer, and certainly not tonight. But it was a fair consideration. They had been together more than a decade. *Is it necessary to dissolve our marriage so quickly?* "What about Tina? Won't she be upset that you're not divorcing your wife in 90 days?" Isabelle put him on the spot.

"Izz, we had one drink," Arnie seemed perplexed. "It was coffee. And we talked about you."

"You talked about me with a skank who clearly set out to ruin our marriage?"

"She said you were friends," Arnie said.

"Wait. Time out. You thought she was my friend and you asked her out?"

"No. We were working out on side-by-side cardio machines at the gym. We were just talking and I realized you worked together. She said you were friends. I probably shouldn't have, but I thought maybe she could help me understand what was going on with you so I asked her if she wanted to grab coffee afterward. To talk about you," Arnie said. It was clear he wasn't making this up.

"So you didn't kiss her? You didn't sleep with her?" Isabelle asked.

"Kiss her. Like on the cheek? Like you just did with Amone? I didn't kiss her romantically and I sure the hell didn't sleep with her," Arnie answered honestly.

Tina had given Isabelle a very different impression.

"But when I asked you at Abby's if you were dating someone, you said we were separated. You led me to believe you had moved on. You forced me to sign divorce papers," Isabelle said.

"I didn't know what you were talking about, and I didn't want to get off track. Look, I don't want to upset you but we had been fighting so much. We were so miserable. I was miserable. I imagined you had to be too. But you've been different lately. It's like you're trying. And it makes me want to try again too," Arnie said.

This was not what Isabelle had in mind. She did not expect to be put on the spot this night of all nights about the entire future of their relationship. She bit her lower lip, out of habit, but which also let him know she was considering his proposal. "You devastated me when you served me divorce papers. And you had it all planned out," she said in such a disappointed tone. "You never plan, but you planned every detail of that."

"No, actually, it seemed that way but I didn't plan any of it. Grace really was supposed to be there. I was going to give you the papers," Arnie said.

Isabelle interrupted, "In front of Grace?"

"No, I was going to send the envelope with you. Just to consider. I don't know. It was a bad idea. It was the only way to let you know how unhappy I had become. I didn't think it out, no matter how it looked. Then, Grace went with a friend and I was meeting you, and it just seemed like a good time," Arnie said.

"A good time?" Isabelle questioned.

"An open window. I don't have the right words. I'm not a writer. I'm not going to always say things the best way. But I'm worried that if we separate now, we may always wonder if we could have made it if we both would have just tried a tiny bit harder. I know I haven't given you my best. I'm sorry. But I want to," Arnie said. He was terrified that she would say it was too late.

In the middle of this crazy cacophony of overhead speakers and music, bright colors and penetrating smells from the chili cook-off, Isabelle and Arnie stood to the side of the room, almost in a bubble, separated from the rampant activity swirling around them. This was the make or break moment, and in their own ways, they were each holding their breath unsure of what the other would say next.

Isabelle wanted to say it was too late, but she didn't. It seemed clear that their base goals were completely different. It seemed so appropriate that Isabelle should feel deprived of support and resentful of Arnie. She just needed to tell him the truth. *I'm sorry, babe. It's just too late.*

Isabelle looked at the colorful basketball lines on the gym floor and shifted her weight from one foot to the other. She was thinking. *What if it's not too late?*

"Okay," Isabelle said. "I'm not going to make any promises other than I will try with you if you will try with me." A voice inside suggested that while he would always be important to her, they might not grow old together. She pushed that voice aside.

Arnie was so happy he started coughing and breathing funny in an excited way as if he expected her to walk away but all the while prayed determinedly she gave them one more chance. He wanted to pinch himself and her to make sure this was really happening. He couldn't stop himself from starting to cry, even though that was the last thing he wanted to do. But aside from a flash moment of hesitation over the unexpected tears, he let out a huge sigh of relief and didn't care who looked over and saw him. He wrapped his arms around Isabelle and pulled her into him. Although she felt more pensive, more reluctant about their future together, she too was happy. She felt like he was fighting hard for her and for them. And while she didn't want to have to pretend to be someone she wasn't, she was willing to make a big effort for their daughter and for the marriage she was sure could not be saved, up until this exact moment. She still wasn't sure, but at least now she was open to it and open to him.

Fifty feet away Amone and Zach were stealing glances, covertly pointing and smiling. Amone winked at Isabelle before she turned and gave Zach a look that indicated *I told you so*, to which Zach returned a surrendering nod. He had to hand it to Amone for her impressive grasp of relationship complexities. There wasn't a day that passed that she didn't take his breath away in one way or another.

Arnie and Isabelle looked up just in time to wave to Grace and let her know they were watching her competition. They quickly returned to their seats with the others where they could have a better view of Grace. She was such a little performer. Ten teams started round one and seven were eliminated due to egg breakage. In round two, another competitor fell short.

In the final round, Grace's partner slipped and her foot crossed a line after the experiment was set up, which gave an automatic win to the other team. It seemed unfair. Arnie and Isabelle both knew their daughter deserved first. Zach yelled out, "Do over," but the judge remained firm. Grace and her partner were awarded red ribbons for second place.

"She ought to take that egg and throw it at the judge," Zach said.

"What a great idea," Isabelle told her brother, joking. *Silly boys.*

"No, don't do that," Harriet said. Isabelle wondered how they would get used to Harriet's cognitive changes following the stroke. She was still Harriet, but some of her was missing. *Would she ever be able to joke around again?* Isabelle would give anything for Harriet to take on the personality of her younger self that Isabelle had become so close the last month. She smiled at her. It was enough for Isabelle to know that her Harriet was inside her aunt somewhere.

Grace ran to her parents. "I only got a red one," she said with a sad tone in her voice.

"Red is my favorite color. May I keep your ribbon?" Isabelle asked her daughter.

"I don't really want it. It wasn't fair," Grace said.

"Sometimes life is completely unfair, kiddo," Isabelle said, drawing her daughter in close. "What do you say we get out of here?"

Zach and Amone offered to take Harriet home and make sure she had her medication and was put to bed comfortably. Grace rode with Isabelle, and Arnie followed them to their house in his car.

At home, Isabelle made Grace's favorite chicken lettuce wraps. She modified a recipe she found online that was supposedly from a well-known chain restaurant. Arnie stopped himself from repeating the cliché, "Get someone hungry enough and anything will taste good."

In that moment, he realized how many jokes he made at Isabelle's expense. He thought they were funny at the time, but each little dig wormed under Isabelle's skin and fostered a wall between them. It hit him that for years these innocent jokes, that he never intended to hurt her feelings, had in fact made her angry. And she retaliated in ways that drove him away.

Their insults – veiled in humor – had damaged their relationship from both sides. Arnie saw that funny lines in a television sitcom weren't that funny in real life when used against someone he loved. And so, instead of cracking a joke, he simply said, "Smells great," as he reached for the cork screw and opened a bottle of late harvest Riesling.

Grace talked nonstop through dinner. She was animated again, like the child they once knew. She may have been given a second place ribbon at school, but what she wanted more than anything was sitting before her right here at home.

At quarter to ten, Isabelle practically gasped when she looked at the clock. "Is it really that late? We're gonna have a tired little girl tomorrow, Arnie."

"I don't want to go to bed, mom. I want to stay up all night," Grace said.

"Hmmm. What do you think your teacher will say when you fall asleep during spelling tomorrow?" Isabelle asked.

"I can sleep at recess?" the little girl negotiated.

"I think your mom knows best on this one, Babe," Arnie backed Isabelle up to Grace. Despite much pleading and begging from Grace, the negotiations finally came to an end and she succumbed to going to bed. Before climbing into the covers, she wrapped her willowy arms around her dad and squeezed him. She held on longer than usual. It was clear she wanted her family back together. She asked for this in as many ways as a child her age could.

"It's only for the night, Honey," Arnie said.

I'm glad we're giving this one more shot. Arnie and Isabelle tucked her in together before both saying goodnight at her bedroom door.

Arnie and Isabelle didn't get down the hall and back to the kitchen before Arnie grabbed her, took her in his arms and kissed her like she longed to be kissed. For all her hesitations over the past twenty-four hours, it felt right to be here with him now.

She expected him to lead her to the bedroom but he didn't. He just kissed her, ran his hands up her toned torso, and showered her with love. He stopped kissing her periodically to gaze longingly and lovingly into her eyes. He told her over and over, "I love you, Izz. This can work. We can be happy again." The more he repeated it, the more possible it seemed.

Even at the school, while she was open to reuniting, she never expected to have such deep feelings rekindled. If she had thought about it, she probably would have pulled away to talk things out or outline a plan on a napkin. But for once, she didn't over-think it. She went with the moment and asked Arnie to make love to her. "I thought you'd never ask." He laughed.

They made love in a way they hadn't for years. They made love the way they once did back when they were young and carefree in San Francisco. And when they were finished, he held her and kissed the side of her face and her hair. She buried her nose in his chest, inhaling the scent of him. She could almost feel them breathe as one.

"Do you want to spend the night?" she asked him playfully, almost exactly the way she once did when they were dating, before they shared a cramped apartment overlooking Portsmouth Square.

"I do, but I need to run home and get some clothes. I have an early meeting and need to scoot out of here by six o'clock. If I leave to get some things, can I come back tonight?" he asked, almost like a lovesick teenager.

She didn't correct his grammar. "Sure," she simply said.

"Don't go anywhere. I'll be back," he said, mimicking Arnold Schwarzenegger in *Terminator*. Arnie jumped out of bed and threw on his clothes. He looked back only to flash her a very large smile, which caused her to smile in return.

Twenty-five minutes later, Isabelle was wondering what was keeping him when her cell phone rang. It was him. "Where are you, Silly?" she asked before he could get a word in first.

It wasn't Arnie. It was his phone. A paramedic was on the other line. She almost dropped the phone.

Everything went into slow motion. It was as if the person on the other end of the phone was talking to her from one end of a very long tunnel and she was on the other end. "Is this Mrs. Salton?" the voice asked.

"Yes, who are you?" she demanded to know who had Arnie's phone.

"There's been an accident. I'm Ron, a paramedic with AMR ambulance service, and your husband is in route to Providence Portland Medical Center. You need to come quickly," the voice said.

"How'd you get his phone?" she asked.

"It was on him. You need to come soon, ma'am. I'm very sorry," Ron said and hung up.

"Hello. Hello. Are you there? Did you hang up on me?" Isabelle was spinning in too many directions. She called Zach.

When he answered, she just talked. She didn't let him get a word in. "Zach, I need you to come watch Grace now. Arnie's been in an accident. I need you to come now," Isabelle was screaming.

"Go. Go to the hospital. Leave your phone on. Turn your ringer on right now. I'm on my way," Zach directed her.

"Okay," Isabelle hung up without telling Zach which hospital. Knowing his sister so well, Zach anticipated this and that was why he specifically told her to leave her phone on. He would call her when she had a chance to get to the hospital, see Arnie and know he was okay. Before Zach could say a word, Amone was out of bed also, coat on and purse in hand ready to go with him to care for Grace.

If only he had clothes at her house. If only he didn't have an early meeting. If only he had gone home before they made love, so he was back and missed the accident altogether. If only they hadn't made love that night. So many *if only* scenarios ran through Isabelle's head as she raced downtown. "I don't pray often, and I don't know if you can hear me, God. But if you can, please let Arnie be okay," she prayed as she sped to the hospital.

CHAPTER 12

I sabelle didn't pay attention to the parking signs when she arrived to the Emergency Department at Providence Portland. She grabbed her purse and ran in. The lady at check-in was on the phone and the others were busy. "I need help. I need help. My husband was brought here from a car accident," she spoke loudly to the admitting clerk.

"Just a minute ma'am," the clerk said.

"I don't have a minute," Isabelle snapped back.

"Are you having chest pain?" the clerk asked.

"No, I need to get to my husband," Isabelle said.

"Just a minute ma'am," the clerk said again.

Security came out and tried to calm Isabelle down. They took her to a quiet room, where she was met by Carrie. Isabelle just started shaking her head and saying, "No, no, no," over and over.

"Isabelle, he's alive. He's fragile and in the trauma room. I need you to bunny-up. Put this on and I'll take you in," Carrie said. Isabelle climbed into a white paper onesie with full arms and legs, like pajamas for a small child only in adults size. It zipped up the front. Carrie handed her a cap for her hair, gloves and booties to cover her shoes. "You need to stay calm," Carrie ordered as she walked her friend down the hall to an ED trauma room.

There was blood everywhere. Arnie was unconscious. It was a bad scene but Isabelle needed to be here. She wished she could thank the paramedic who called her. She was glad that Arnie hadn't followed her advice and put a code on his phone. She told him anyone who accessed his phone could get right into his contacts. *Thank God he hadn't listened to me. Thank God for Ron.* She would never forget that paramedic's name.

"Dr. Hoyt," one of the nurses said in a tone that questioned Carrie for bringing in a family member.

"She's his wife and a close family friend. She needs to be here. She'll be okay," Carrie assured the team. Isabelle wasn't going to let her friend down.

"Can I talk to him? Can he hear me?" Isabelle asked Carrie. Carrie positioned Isabelle so she would be close but not in the way of the trauma and rapid response teams.

"Arnie, it's Isabelle. I'm here. You're going to be okay. You were in a car accident but you're going to be okay. I love you. I love you. You're going to be okay. I love you, Arnie," Isabelle said before her legs buckled and she slipped backward into the wall.

"Okay, I need to get you out of here right now. I can bring you back in later, but you need to come with me right now, okay. Come on, please," Carrie took her hand and led her back to a private room.

"Where am I? Where are you taking me?" Isabelle asked. Carrie took her to a special office with a desk, a bed and a television.

"It's our physician break room. Do you want the television on?" Carrie asked.

"No," Isabelle said. "Thank you," she whispered. Isabelle felt as if her life was suddenly surrounded by a fog machine, with clouds that made it impossible to see, and funny smells and sounds.

Carrie treated Isabelle the way she would have treated her own sister, if she had one. As an only child, she could only hope her response in Isabelle's time of need was indeed what she needed to cope. Despite the mad circumstances of the moment, for just a second Isabelle could feel firsthand the tenderness Carrie had directed toward Harriet for years. Only someone with the purest intentions could respond so intimately and affectionately in such a vulnerable and life-changing moment. Carrie would always be family no matter how this episode played out.

"Okay, lie down and rest. I will come back for you. Do not leave this room. Wait for me here, no matter how long it takes, okay?" Dr. Hoyt confirmed.

"Okay, Carrie. Okay," Isabelle said before lying down and blacking out.

FIVE MONTHS LATER – MAUI, HAWAII

A pile of suitcases had been dropped off in their condominium at the Sands of Kahana in West Maui. Grace was unpacking her small suitcase that Isabelle allowed her to pull behind her in the room she shared with Harriet. The bedroom Grace was sharing with Harriet had two queen beds, which made Grace definitely feel like a big girl. The condominium unit was large and Isabelle was in the master bedroom, which included a deck that faced the Pacific Ocean.

Arnie was sitting on the lanai when Isabelle walked outside in a long flowing Hawaiian dress. Her long hair was pulled back in a ponytail so it didn't fall forward when she leaned her arms on the rail. "We were always going to come back here together," Arnie said.

"We were always going to come back here together," she

repeated his words as she stared ahead at the waves. There was a knock at the door. Isabelle turned to walk across the condo but Grace beat her to it. It was Zach.

"How's the digs?" Zach asked.

Isabelle laughed when he said that. She had learned to relax so much in the last five months. It took her forty years to discern which battles were worth fighting, but this past year she changed a lifetime in a matter of months. And it truly helped her relationships – all of her relationships, when she was able to let go a little and stop trying to control the world around her. "I missed this place," Isabelle said. "Frank and Harriet brought us to the Sands the year it opened, when you were in college and I was a senior in high school," she reminded her brother.

"That feels like a lifetime ago," he said.

"It does. Has Carrie arrived? What about Richard?" she asked.

"No, just us. Richard is arriving in an hour at Kapalua. Do you remember that time you went walking out on the runway to take pictures?" Zach started laughing. "Oh man. There was a Cessna coming in and the airport staff was yelling at you to come back. And there you stood, just taking picture after picture," Zach snorted as he bent over laughing. "You were crazy."

She smiled at the memory. "I just wanted a picture of the airport from the tarmac and I found a better angle when I backed up a little," Isabelle said.

"You're an idiot. You walked out onto the runway with a plane coming in." Zach laughed.

"I was trying to get the perfect shot," Isabelle defended her actions two decades later.

"It's funny now. If you had done that after nine-eleven you probably would have landed back in jail in Kahului," Zach said. "I would have wanted a picture of that."

"Probably. I didn't think about anything but getting a good picture at the time," Isabelle said, playing along. Zach stopped laughing and got serious all of a sudden.

"Are you sure you're okay with this? Combining our wedding and Arnie's celebration of life in one trip?" Zach asked. He was genuinely worried that it might be too overwhelming for Isabelle to do both within a few days of each other.

"It's what he would have wanted," Isabelle said. "Plus, it just made the best sense logistically. Who knows, maybe Robert and his family will stay for the wedding. God knows we're going to need all the family we can get around us to manage."

"If you change your mind, I will understand," Zach said.

"You want to put your wedding off?" Isabelle said jokingly. "Amone will love that."

"No. But we would if you needed us to. I would. And she would understand," Zach said. Isabelle was amazed how close she and Zach, and Amone, had become the last five months since Arnie's passing. She wasn't sure she and Grace could have gotten through it without them. They were a tremendous support. Zach and Amone would make it official in a few days but she was already a proven sister to Isabelle and aunt to Grace. She was family.

"I know. Hey, we're running down to the Honokowai Market for some groceries. Wanna come?" Isabelle asked.

"Sure. Let me text Amone that I'm going with you. Are Harriet and Grace coming?" Zach asked.

"Yes. Harriet loves the farmer's market and I like to let Grace pick out fresh fruits and vegetables. It creates buy-in when she picks them out," Isabelle conceded.

"Awe. Yes," Zach nodded.

"Harriet, Grace, do you want to go to the farmer's market?" Isabelle called into the other room from the kitchen.

"Which one are you going to?" Harriet asked?

"The outdoor one on the Lower Honoapiilani Road," Isabelle confirmed.

"It's not open now. It's only open on Monday, Wednesday and Fridays from seven to eleven," Harriet said walking into the dining room. Isabelle was continually surprised and impressed how well Harriet had come back from her stroke. Her speech was nearly perfect and her memory was impressive. It really did feel like a miracle in many ways. Isabelle wished Arnie could be here too. *It would have been so wonderful to have everyone together for Zach and Amone's wedding.*

"We'll just go to the store portion for some things and catch the outdoor market tomorrow," Isabelle said. Zach, Isabelle, Grace and Harriet loaded into the car and took off for the market. Despite the busy park across the street, there was an open parking space right up front. Isabelle smiled with a surprised sense of unexpected gratitude. On days the outdoor market was set up, it was not uncommon to drive in circles and still park a couple of blocks away.

Once inside, Harriet gave Isabelle direction on picking out avocados and reiterated that since they were priced individually, Isabelle should weigh all of them to make sure she was getting the best value. Things like this once drove Isabelle mad, but no longer. She knew Harriet's intention was to help – and she had learned in their time together that helping was truly what Harriet most wanted to give to any relationship. Harriet took the bunch of bananas Isabelle was holding out of her hands and redirected her to the ripened bananas to her right.

Harriet had a good point. With so many people in their party and the market being so close, they might as well just buy what they needed each day. Isabelle laughed to herself when she thought about how glad she was that Harriet didn't always go grocery shopping with her. But this was a special occasion, a time they would always remember as a family, and Isabelle was going to give Harriet the grace to be herself without subduing her for one whole week. In the meantime, Grace managed to fill a shopping cart with enough food for several weeks, so Isabelle stepped in to negotiate. "I don't think we're going to need three boxes of cereal for one week. How about if you pick one," Isabelle redirected.

"But I like all of them and we're on vacation," Grace said. Isabelle felt a brush of air move past her. That was exactly the kind of logic Arnie would have used, and had used many times. How could Isabelle refuse this request?

"You can have all of them, but only one at a time. So pick which one you want first and when the box is gone you can pick whichever one you want next," Isabelle explained.

"Okay," Grace reluctantly conceded. "This one." Grace held up Lucky Charms. It was Arnie's favorite too. She had gone in rounds with him about setting a bad example for their daughter. But today, she just laughed. In a way, she was thankful for moments like these. They would remind her that he would always be an important part of their lives. He would live on through Grace, and the child Isabelle was carrying from the night the car accident took him away.

Zach stepped in as the voice of reason. "We probably should check out soon. Robert's landing in fifteen minutes."

"Will his stuff fit in the car with all of us or do we need to pick up a second car?" Isabelle asked.

"Well, I don't know if he's coming alone, but we pretty much fill up the car, and we're buying groceries. We need to pick up a second car if we're all going to meet him. Or I can just pick him up and meet back at the Sands," Zach said.

"Why don't I make lunch and you pick him up? Is that okay? Do you want to take Grace or leave her with me?" Isabelle asked.

"Whatever she wants," Zach said. *Of course he would leave the decision to a child.*

Isabelle shrugged and replied, "Sounds good." Arnie would not believe how relaxed she had become. *He wouldn't even recognize me.*

◆ ◆ ◆

When Zach returned with Robert and Grace, he had one more child along. Robert's daughter Pinky was a year younger than Grace. Isabelle had only met Arnie's brother Robert once, the only time she and Arnie went to Hawaii together. Robert lived on Oahu. He had been stationed there and transitioned to private citizenship after he retired from the Army.

Robert went through some difficult times on multiple tours to the Middle East, tours that changed him, made him less social and less inclined to connect and communicate with Arnie. Isabelle was never sure if Robert had told Arnie what happened or if Arnie had failed to pass that information on to her. All she knew was that Robert and Arnie rarely talked and Arnie almost never mentioned his brother to her. It was a sore subject and one Isabelle learned not to bring up.

Part of selecting Hawaii to spread Arnie's ashes was Isabelle's hope to provide a way for Robert to participate. He was never able to make it back to the mainland, and Isabelle felt this might be one last gift to the man she loved, to have his brother at his celebration of life. She always wished her life with Arnie would have been filled with an extended family of cousins and kids gathering to celebrate the seasons in local parks and planning family reunions together.

So to see Robert walk in with Pinky in many ways was a twisted version of the daydream she held in her mind. As Isabelle made lunch, Harriet stood close making suggestions for how Isabelle could improve each process. It reminded Isabelle of growing up in Harriet's home when Isabelle always thought Harriet talked to her that way because she still considered her a child. Isabelle's mind briefly flashed to an alternate scenario – one in which Harriet didn't recover, didn't come home, and wasn't able to monitor her most mundane activities. Isabelle was only too happy to be told she put the silverware in the dishwasher the wrong direction given the alternative that Harriet didn't come home.

"Now how did you get the name Pinky?" Harriet asked Robert's daughter.

"It's always been my name," the little girl said.

"Her mother named her Penelope Rae and she just seems more like a Pinky," Robert piped up.

"Well that's very strange," Harriet said. Isabelle worried that with Robert already being so gun-shy about family that unintentionally Harriet might offend him and drive him away forever.

"She means well," Isabelle leaned in and said to Robert.

"I can hear you and I don't need you to speak for me. I can speak for myself. Can't I say what I think without being shushed or ignored?" Harriet asked. Grace and Pinky ran off to play in the other room. There was a knock on the door. It was Amone.

"I can tell you have a great spirit," Robert graciously continued his conversation with Harriet. "We've all walked on eggshells far too long in this family." Robert winked. Isabelle felt instant relief. "Pinky is a fun, strange little name," Robert said. "But it beats Penelope Rae. That's way too big of a name for a little girl."

"Well, it gives her something to grow into," Harriet argued.

"I think it's cute. It might be something that sticks. You never know," Isabelle added. "Okay, who's ready for lunch? I did everything family style so folks could just take what they want."

The gourmet kitchen was busy with a growing family. Isabelle breathed in deeply thinking of Arnie. If only he could have been here with the group. She was sure he would have enjoyed being part of a big, loud family, even if he didn't see it years ago when she first told him it was all she really wanted in life – to belong to something bigger than herself.

There was another knock on the door. It was Carrie. Isabelle would never forget the way she cared for Arnie on his last night, and more importantly cared for her when she couldn't care for herself. Carrie had truly become the sister Isabelle never had.

Carrie made her round of hugs. She may not have been family by blood, but she was every bit family through friendship and love. The family wasn't complete until she arrived.

Zach and Robert took plates out to the waterfront lanai. The condo had two decks, each with tables and chairs, creating enough room for everyone to sit comfortably. While Carrie was catching up with Harriet and Amone, Isabelle joined Zach and Robert on the lanai.

She knew Arnie wasn't physically there, but she could feel his presence as if he were sitting right there with them. She felt his spirit very much alive.

Isabelle was never able to see Arnie's spirit, but she continually felt his presence. She even talked to him sometimes as home. She wondered if he might someday come to her the way Harriet did when she had her stroke. *Wouldn't that be wonderful?* A part of her wanted to chase everyone out, just to see, but she didn't. There would be time for that.

Robert and Zach were catching up like no time had ever passed since they met at Arnie and Isabelle's wedding – before everyone went their own ways and life got crunchy and complicated. Isabelle was amazed how different the conversation between the men was than if they had been two women. There was no reminiscing or either one asking how they let time go by. In fact, they were talking about renting a fishing charter out of Lahaina to see if they could bring home a marlin. Isabelle couldn't see Amone allowing a big stuffed fish to hang on the wall in her home. And as soon as they finished the conversation about fishing they segued directly into baseball.

"This is why men can jump right back into a relationship with someone you haven't seen in years because you avoid talking about sensitive things and unresolved feelings," Isabelle chimed in. Both men stopped and looked at her with blank stares on their faces.

Zach let out the smallest, "Huh?" before Robert jumped right back in about the starting pitchers in the American League. Oregon didn't have a professional baseball team so Isabelle was confused why they cared so much about baseball when the Timbers were already practicing and both of them actually played soccer in high school. She could tell that she had clearly crashed a conversation that was beyond her scope of input, so she sat and listened for a few minutes until she got up and walked back inside.

CHAPTER 13

J ust before sunset, the horn sounded to alert the resort. Vacationers and kama 'ainas alike made their way to the shore. At sunset, large groups gathered to watch the sun slide down behind the water and sister islands in the distance. But within minutes of the sun setting, most people returned to their condos, the steel barbecue pits set in stone throughout the resort, the pool or the restaurant and bar overlooking the pool to start dinner or get back on with their lives.

Isabelle, with Grace by her side, held a small urn of Arnie's ashes. She took a deep breath. She had thought about this moment so many times but had not anticipated the enormity of it until it finally arrived. Isabelle chose a dress for this occasion that showed her baby-bump in a way that was significantly more apparent than in the dress she wore earlier that day.

She thought about the things she wanted to say, the things she should say, and the things she wasn't sure she wanted her daughter to hear. But in the end, everything blended together as she took a deep breath and began to speak. Off to the side, watching her with a bright spirit and open heart was the man whose life they gathered to celebrate and honor. He was always proud of her but never more so than in that moment, doing what he was so glad he never had to do – say goodbye to the love of his life. She couldn't see him, but she felt his presence and he had a perfect view of her.

"Carl Jung once said, 'The meeting of two personalities is like the contact of two chemical substances. If there is any re-action, both are transformed.' We were all transformed by the man whose life we celebrate today – Arnold David Salton. No matter how much time you have with someone you love, it is never enough," Isabelle began. "If we were given one more day, we would undoubtedly ask again for yet one more day. Arnie, thank you for every day I had with you. I know I never said thank you enough. But I am more grateful than I could ever say for that scrawny, scruffy man-child who walked into my life in San Francisco and gave me an E-ticket for a ride beyond my wildest imagination.

"Arnie and I didn't always have an easy relationship. Are any relationships with other imperfect humans easy? They all start out easy – when we meet someone and we're all excited and forward-looking – giving that other person the best of ourselves every moment. New loves and new friendships are always fun and thrilling. But then we get comfortable and we settle into daily routines and outside stressors. People get on our nerves. They push our buttons. Our dreams get banged up and the full kaleidoscope of our personalities shines through. Some views have sharp colors and rough edges; others are more pleasing. But something else happens in long-term relationships, we somehow get through things that new relationships could never withstand.

"Arnie was the love of my life. He opened up a new world of possibilities and experiences. He gave me two amazing children – our daughter Grace and this little bundle of, uh, I was going to say morning sickness but thankfully that's gone away. Bundle of hope. I don't know, Grace, if you're going to have a sister or a brother. Your dad made me wait to find out with you, so for him, we're waiting a few more months on this one too. We're doing that for daddy.

"Arnie drove me crazy. We were so different. In many

ways, Arnie was the big kid in my life who never grew up, who kept me young, and ultimately taught me to stop taking all the little things so darn seriously and trying to, as he would say, control the weather. For the record, I never tried to control the weather." Isabelle laughed at this, which broke some tension, and in doing so gave everyone else permission to do the same.

"Arnie, we always said we'd come back here together. But life is busy and short and in honor of your life, starting today we're throwing all our good intentions out the window. In honor of you, I'm going to make the time to invest in creating new memories with the people we love. In celebration of your life, we are going to live. We are not going to dream. We are going to do. We are going to parasail and surf again. We are going to get up at three o'clock in the morning and bike down Haleakala. I'm going to get the scuba certification we always talked about before we return next year. We are going to return next year, and the year after, and the year after that. We are going to live and we are going to do everything we can while we still can – here.

"I would give anything for one more day with you. But instead, I'm going to take the lessons you taught me and hold tightly to our babies and treasure the days I have with them, with Zach and Amone, Harriet, Richard, Pinky and Carrie. We are all going to celebrate life – Arnie's life and our lives together.

"Arnie, we may have had our differences, but you were my lifeline in this world. God knows I'm so especially thankful for our last day together. That was a perfect day, really. I'm thankful for the family we made together – and for our extended family, which has been here for us every day since." Isabelle paused, looked down at the sand, and then unexpectedly laughed before continuing.

"Earlier today," Isabelle stopped speaking, as if she might not go on. But after taking a deep breath, she continued. "Grace wanted three boxes of cereal – for one week here in Maui. That was totally something you would have done – buy three different boxes of cereal for seven days on an island." She shook her head slowly side-to-side. Tears trickled in a steady stream down her cheek. She took her hand and wiped them away, and then placed her hand on her heart as if she were going to pledge to a flag.

"Every day, she seems to do or say something funny or re-markable that reminds me that you are always with us," Isabelle stopped, smiled and repeated herself. "You are always with us, because you will forever be in our hearts. You will forever be in the eyes of our children. The things you made or tried to fix will forever be in our home. You will forever impact me. You will forever be part of all of us."

Isabelle looked up at the sky. She tipped her head back and used her right hand as a visor as if to shield her eyes.

"I release you, Arnie. To God and the angels. You were only on loan to me. We are all only on loan to each other. It is up to us to take care of ourselves and the beautiful spirits on loan to us, one day at a time because that is all we ever have." Everyone ex-cept for Isabelle stood silently and motionless, not even mov-ing a hand to wipe tears, despite the fact they all had them. "I love you, Babe. My heart is with you always," Isabelle said as she reached down to tenderly take Grace's hand in her own. Grace looked up to her mom for comfort, with her deep, soulful eyes protected only by her long dark lashes.

Isabelle walked with her daughter to the shoreline, and together they stepped into the foamy crashing waves as the others stood back and clasped their hands together at the crest of the sand. They walked out several feet into thigh high water. Isabelle, with Grace at her side, took handful after handful of ash and placed it on the surface of the water, letting the move-ment of the sea embrace into the bluish-green water what they had left of Arnie. There was a small amount left and Isabelle considered dumping it out, but something stopped her. There was one more thing she still needed to do – for herself and to honor the time on earth they shared. And so with a deeply inhaled sigh, she closed the lid.

Isabelle turned and picked up her crying Grace from the sea. She held her, hearts facing, and silently comforted her as they returned to the others waiting, twenty-five feet away. They might as well have been five hundred feet or five hundred miles. It was the longest walk for Isabelle, leaving Arnie's ashes in the sea and returning without him to land.

Isabelle and Grace were welcomed by love and open arms. Arnie had given her the loving family she always wanted. She could feel his presence with them. Isabelle was filled with a sense of peace and protection. She didn't know how they would be okay, but instinctively, she knew they would.

The next two days on Maui were cool, dark and wet. Maui seldom saw extended weather like this. Isabelle embraced it. She felt as if the skies were mourning with her. Somehow it wouldn't have seemed as appropriate to release Arnie and immediately return to the happy, breezy paradise life she always associated with the islands.

At one point, Zach and Amone offered to postpone their vows if Isabelle didn't mind a second trip to Maui – their treat. *We've come so far in less than half a year.* Over the past six months, Isabelle had taken to speaking and reacting less and thinking much more. Enough so that when she just smiled at this offer, they originally misunderstood and started calling off arrangements.

When news of this made its way back to her, she had to pick up the phone and insist they proceed with the original plans. *Arnie always loved a party.* Isabelle insisted that proceeding as planned is what Arnie would have wanted – and what she wanted as well.

The next morning started hazy but clouds cleared and the sun quickly came out. It was time to celebrate – with a fun, memorable, Hawaiian beach wedding.

With the ceremony a day away, Isabelle decided to surprise Amone. The last time they had spent any real time together one-on-one was when they both showed up to hike the falls. This adventure would mark a fresh beginning. Isabelle first asked Harriet if she would mind watching Grace and Pinky, before she called Zach and ran her idea past him.

Zach loved how close Isabelle and Amone had become, and that Isabelle was reaching out to his soon-to-be wife. "Please don't get her killed," he said, jokingly.

"Just her? Not me?" Isabelle playfully challenged him.

"I need you both to return in good condition," he confirmed. Isabelle's eyes started to tear up, but she didn't let him know how much his words had affected her. *It's probably these stupid hormones making me so emotional.* Over the past months, her relationship with Zach had come full circle to the brother who once fiercely protected her. Here she was, a woman living without two of the men she never expected to lose too soon – her dad and then her husband. But she still had a great guardian and defender in Zach, and she no longer took him for granted the way she once had.

With Zach on board, Isabelle was able to convince Amone to throw on a bathing suit and meet her at the car. "You're not going to tell me where you're taking me are you?" Amone asked.

"Nope," Isabelle said, tossing her head back as she laughed.

"Man, between you and your brother, I am not going to stand a chance," Amone said, once inside the car.

Isabelle gave no clues along the way. In fact, she turned

left onto the highway to initially throw Amone off that they were even headed toward Lahaina. Once they got up to Napili Market, Isabelle said, "I need to run in for something. Do you wanna come?"

Amone was completely unsure where this was going, so out of curiosity she immediately jumped out of the car to tag along. Isabelle picked up two bottles of chilled water, a can of salted cashews and a bag of frozen peas. Amone knew immediately what Isabelle had in mind, and she was so excited. It had been years since she had been snorkeling.

"I love you," Amone leaned in and whispered.

Isabelle was hoping, counting on even, that Zach had at some point shared their family secret about snorkeling with Amone. Frozen peas. Zach and Isabelle learned about this little island trick years ago, on their first family trip to Maui. They were shocked the first time they were swarmed by tropical fish as the then adolescent kids released handfuls of the green vegetables into the blue water. So out of her desire to keep her future sister-in-law guessing, Isabelle bought one bag of frozen peas.

When the ladies got back to the car, and buckled their seatbelts, Isabelle turned to Amone and smiled. "And we're off," she said.

"Oh gosh, how long will we be?" Amone asked. "I forgot I was meeting the resort event planner this afternoon to go through some basic rehearsal walk-through stuff for tomorrow."

"An hour, an hour and a half, and another hour," Isabelle talked aloud as she was thinking. "I'd say we will be back by fourish, but no later than six."

"Oh. I better call Zach and share the good news with him. He's going to need to stand in for me," Amone said sarcastically.

Zach was not thrilled to hear that he now got the pleasure of meeting with the wedding planner alone. Isabelle was laughing inside thinking how much this must be torturing him. He couldn't really be upset with the ladies though as Isabelle knew nothing about the appointment and Amone knew nothing about Isabelle's surprise. He was a good sport and agreed to stand in.

"Okay then, I guess I'll see you at the luau tonight, if not before," Amone wrapped up. "I love you too."

Isabelle did not have snorkeling in mind. Mostly, because she would have taken Grace and Pinky with them for that. But she did want Amone to think they were going snorkeling.

Just as they got to Lahaina Harbor, a car was pulling out of a four-hour parking spot. *This never happens!*

"Wow! What great luck!" Amone exclaimed.

"I was just thinking that same thing."

Amone grabbed her purse and small bag with a towel. "I love snorkeling," she said.

"That's awesome. Too bad we're not going snorkeling today," Isabelle said.

"I know we're going snorkeling because you bought the peas," Amone said. "Zach told me about your little island secret."

"I was hoping he would," Isabelle said. She took off toward one of the snorkeling boats and Amone followed her.

"I see we're not snorkeling today," Amone laughed. She was more convinced now than ever that they were in fact snorkeling. Feeling perplexed, she wrinkled her nose and shrugged.

"Nope." Isabelle walked up to two teenage girls waiting for their tour to start and inquired if they were going snorkeling. They nodded and Isabelle handed one of them her bag of mostly frozen peas. Amone wasn't sure what to think when she saw this. "Feed these to the fish slowly, only a few at a time, and you'll have a snorkeling experience to remember," Isabelle told them.

They seemed confused by Isabelle, but smiled nervously, accepted the peas and said thank you.

Isabelle turned to walk away. Amone followed, "So we're not snorkeling," Amone said. "So what are we doing today?" she asked.

"I thought you'd never ask," Isabelle laughed.

"I've been asking."

Isabelle stopped in front of a boat that said Extreme Parasailing. She put her left arm out as if she were a game show model displaying a prize.

"No. Really?" Amone said, almost squealing. *OMG she squeals!* Isabelle had never heard Amone squeal in delight like this.

"Really," Isabelle said nonchalantly, but very proud of herself all the same.

"Does Zach know?"

"Of course not. I told him we were snorkeling," Isabelle laughed. He'll find out when we post the pictures on Facebook.

"You know he never checks Facebook." Amone looked at the parasailing boat, an Ocean Pro 31, slightly smaller than the larger vessel she and Zach almost took a few months back in Florida. "I've always wanted to do this," she giggled.

"Well we're gonna today. Life is short and we're gonna enjoy it."

"Is this safe, when you're pregnant?"

"I would not risk this child. You and me maybe, but not the child. I'm kidding. We're fine."

"Have you ever seen the forms we have to sign to go out on this excursion?" Amone asked.

"Every activity has some sort of liability release forms. It's just part of the deal."

"Zach and I were planning to go when we were in Tampa right after Christmas. He read the release form and convinced me it was too dangerous. And Zach's not easily spooked. He loves danger." It amazed Isabelle to hear stories of Zach making decisions out of fear given the risk-taking side of himself he always showed her.

"If you don't want to go we can cancel. But I really think we're safe. I think it will be fun," Isabelle said. She could see Amone debating. "Listen, you guys were in Florida a few months after Arnie died – and a few months after the high profile parasailing accidents in Florida that had been on the news. It's understandable, but these really are safe."

Isabelle wasn't sure if Amone was going to back out. *Maybe I should have stuck with snorkeling.* She didn't want to pressure her, but she really wanted to go. She wanted to keep the promise she made at Arnie's celebration of life to live – really live – not just half-heartedly go about life.

"Let's do it," Amone decided. Not three seconds later a tour operator walked up to them, checked their names off a list and handed them a daunting liability release form.

Isabelle's eyes got big when she read the first few paragraphs. "See, I told you," Amone said.

"I thought Zach was being a wussy, but I can see how this would freak someone out," Isabelle conceded. "It kinda freaks me out. Oh what the heck," Isabelle said, turning the paper over and signing it without reading the rest of the small print.

The women hopped aboard with the other six people who had registered. Everyone was required to wear lifejackets and instructed to remain seated while in route to the open water. The crew gave specific instructions on safety procedures and noted when it was safe to move about the boat.

As the speedboat jetted out to the open water, saltwater sprayed up from the sides of the boat and back toward the deep wake that had formed behind the vessel. The wind whipped through their hair. Amone mouthed to Isabelle, "This is fun. Thank you."

When they arrived to the destination, miles of clear open water, Isabelle and Amone leaned together for a selfie which Isabelle immediately posted to Instagram. "You posted that?" Amone asked.

"I doubt Zach even knows what Instagram is," said Isabelle.

"Oh but Pinky and Grace do," Amone reminded.

"Oops! I bet he'll still marry you," Isabelle laughed.

"It's not me you need to be worried about. You're the one who told him we were going snorkeling."

"He told you. That little blabber mouth. I'm glad I lied to him!"

"No. He told me the pea story a while back. I assumed you told him we were going snorkeling. You had to have told him something and I'm certain you didn't tell him this and he still let us go," Amone said.

"Let us go? What are we, his kids?" Isabelle teased.

"Oh, he wouldn't have said no. He would have simply taken the sparkplugs out of the car or let the air out of the tire. He never says no," Amone joked.

"Look, we're going to be fine. We're going to be better than fine. We're going to have an awesome time and have great memories," Isabelle reassured.

It was Isabelle and Amone's turn to go up. They decided to ride tandem. They had a choice of triple, tandem or single shot rides. Isabelle handed her camera to a lady sitting next to them and asked her to take a few shots. "Do you want a wet landing or a dry landing?" the crew member asked the ladies.

"Wet!" Isabelle immediately replied without giving Amone a chance to weigh in. Going third, they had the advantage of seeing that even a wet landing only got their feet, legs and a small portion of their torso wet. It didn't submerge them in the ocean.

"I think we should go for it," Amone agreed.

Up in the air, the view was spectacular. Lahaina was a tiny hub of activity far off in the distance. Sitting in the harness was almost like sitting in a giant swing, high above the world. Above the boat, the water, the fish and everything living in the ocean below. The light winds tossed them around gently like a balloon on the end of a string. A few birds flew by, about ten feet below them, between their feet and the water.

Isabelle took her hands off the stabilizing ropes and unfolded them wide to embrace a great big world ahead. Amone enjoyed the ride but more cautiously held on. As with every spectacular experience in life, they savored each minute, predicting correctly that just as with life, the ride would be over far too quickly.

As they hovered about thirty feet above the water, Isabelle held onto her stabilizing rope with her right hand and reached over with her left hand to take Amone's right hand. After initially resisting to let go, Amone held Isabelle's left hand in her right. Isabelle forced their hands straight up in the air toward the sky. "We made it," Isabelle said.

"We did," Amone said. "And what a ride it was." Just then they hovered over the water as the lift dunked them just below their waists. The water was so refreshing. Isabelle kicked her feet about like a child playing in a puddle. In less than a minute they were back in the air just far enough to be returned to a dry landing on the deck of the boat.

"So what did you think?" a crew member asked.

"Awesome!" Amone said.

"I wanted to go snorkeling but she talked me into this," Isabelle told the mate, winking at Amone.

"This was really super awesome," Amone said. "Thank you."

"Thank you," Isabelle said to the boat mate. "And thank you, for trusting me," she said to Amone. It went unspoken that they would trust each other for many years to come. It was clear they both realized that sometimes it's the unlikeliest friendships that build the bonds that ultimately last a lifetime.

"I sort of feel bad that we didn't invite Carrie and Harriet to join us," Amone said.

"I know. But I wanted you all to myself this afternoon. Is that terrible?" Isabelle asked.

"No. I'm glad you did."

When the ladies arrived back at the resort, Zach greeted Amone with a kiss and a questioning look that let her know he knew where they had been. Seeing the look on his face, Isabelle jumped in to take the blame. "It was my fault. At the last minute, parasailing just sounded more fun and I didn't know you were opposed to it until we were already on the boat and saw how safe it was."

"Hmm." was all Zach said.

"How did you know?" Isabelle asked.

"You posted it on Instagram," he said, as if it was obvious.

"Who showed you? Did my little Gracie rat me out?" Isabelle asked.

"No," Zach said.

"Pinky?"

"No."

"Carrie?" Isabelle was very surprised that Carrie would do that.

"No. You're running out of people." Zach said.

"I'm also running out of ideas," Isabelle said.

"I did," Harriet said, owning it.

"You're on Instagram?" Carrie and Isabelle asked at exactly the same time.

"Well, I had a long recovery. I had to do something to occupy myself," Harriet said. Harriet was capable of change after all.

"You got me," Isabelle said, laughing and shrugging. "Who knew?"

"Me too," Carrie chimed in.

"Well," Zach said and paused, turning to Amone with a stiff bottom lip. "Did you have fun?"

"Time of my life," she said.

"Great," he said, wrapping his arms around her. "But next time my sister tries to talk you into something crazy..."

"I'm probably going to go for it. We kinda all promised we would." Amone said.

Zach stopped and looked down. Then he looked up and into her eyes, "Yes, we all kinda did. Okay then." Turning to the group he said, "Well, I'm ready for a luau. How fast do you think you gals can change and get ready?"

"Probably faster if you don't follow me," Amone said as she started walking backward toward their condo.

"I'll give ya a head start," he said with a laugh.

"Should we meet back here or over at our place?" Isabelle asked.

"Let's just meet at the luau in an hour." Zach threw out. Everyone agreed and went their separate ways.

Down on the grass, between the restaurant and the tennis courts, the staff had transformed the area into a full-scale, traditional, Hawaiian luau, complete with male and female hula dancers and a feast bursting with fruit buffets, exotic salads, lomilomi salmon, chicken long rice, kalua pork – and poi, which both Zach and Isabelle hated, but convinced the others to try. It was a beautiful blend of Hawaiian, Polynesian and Asian-influenced flavors.

Tiki torches lined the parameter and the sounds of Queen Lili'uokalani blared out from the speakers strategically placed throughout the grounds. Zach and Amone's wedding was anything but traditional, but Isabelle couldn't help but think: *This is the most freaking awesome rehearsal dinner ever.* She was going to mention it but thought maybe not given the fact that it might remind Zach that he got stuck meeting with the wedding planner while she and Amone were out having fun on the boat.

Isabelle found a seat at the table next to Carrie, who was sitting next to Harriet. "You look so beautiful," Isabelle said, leaning over to Carrie.

"Mahalo," Carrie said, in place of thank you.

"Did I see Robert checking you out from the corner of my eye earlier?" Isabelle asked, hinting of a possible spark between Arnie's brother and the good doctor.

"He's got a lot going on in his head," Carrie said.

"Maybe you could help him with some of that," Isabelle suggested.

"Well, he'd be one of my prettier patients, that's for sure," Carrie said smiling.

"Maybe just play doctor instead of being his doctor?" Isabelle whispered. Carrie turned to Isabelle as her jaw dropped.

"IzzyB!?" Carrie exclaimed. "I just met him."

"Give yourself a couple mai tais, and maybe a few slow dances later – you never know. You know what they say," Isabelle teased.

"No. What do they say?" Carrie asked.

"What happens in Maui stays in Maui."

"That's Vegas, and I think you've had one too many mai tais my friend," Carrie said and both gals laughed.

"Yes, that's it!" Isabelle said, pointing to her baby bump. "I've been downing them all week."

"Sorry," Carrie said. "They can make them virgin," Carrie offered.

"I'm good with my club soda," Isabelle said.

Just then Robert returned from the buffet table with his plate. "Can I get anyone anything while I'm still up?" he asked the table but focused his question toward Carrie. Isabelle wanted to nudge her with an elbow, but she didn't want to ruin anything. In looking at them together, something in Isabelle told herself to be cool and let life unfold how it would. *I think he could really be good for her, and vice versa.* Isabelle didn't want to mess up some potential happiness, even down the line, with an ill-placed joke. Isabelle knew the transformational power of love, and she didn't want to even risk spoiling the possibility of it for anyone else.

After eating barely more than Jello and a few bites of rice

and pulled pork, Grace and Pinky were ready to run about. Sitting at long tables of food may have been fine for the adults but the girls were only too happy to join the other kids at the resort in a game of tag and hide and go seek.

Midway through dinner the entertainment got underway. The hula dancers performed together and then spread about, dancing between the tables. At one point the twirling and hip movements resulted in a grass skirt flying up and brushing Robert on the back of his neck. He turned bright red. *I think he might be hot for a little action.* Isabelle bit her lip. She looked over and could see Carrie was intentionally pretending not to notice.

Isabelle asked Robert to dance and when they drew in close she suggested he get to know Carrie a little better. "If you could have seen how amazing she was with Arnie, for that alone you would love her forever," Isabelle told her brother-in-law. "She's a great gal. You should at least get to know her," Isabelle suggested.

Robert did not commit, but Isabelle could tell her suggestion had been heard. When they walked back to the table, Isabelle announced, "Being pregnant, I just don't have the same energy I'm used to." This was Robert's cue to jump in.

"Would you like to pick up where Isabelle fizzled on me?" Robert asked Carrie. This was wildly out of character for Robert, but the combination of Hawaiian rum and a pep talk from Isabelle was just enough to nudge him to make a move.

Carrie looked up at him, her long eyelashes fluttering. "I'd like that," she said, standing up before he had a chance to change his mind. It was the first step in a great dance.

Isabelle watched her loved ones talk, laugh, dance, run, and live in perfect harmony. *Life is good. No. Life is great.*

If only Arnie were here, this would have been a perfect day. Isabelle watched the festivities around her, almost taking place in slow motion and all at once without any sound. Harriet was telling a story as Amone and Zach graciously listened. Carrie was dancing with Robert. Gracie and Pinky were off playing.

Isabelle was anything but alone. She reached into her pocket and felt the tiny sandwich bag with her fingers. It was a perfect day. It was time. Isabelle stood up. She knew what she needed to do.

As she walked toward the water, she could see Arnie. He was leaning against the trunk of a palm tree. He was looking at her the way he did the day she walked down the aisle to meet him at the front of the church. She wanted to run to him that day, but she kept her cadence in step with the traditional wedding day march.

Not now. Not tonight. Isabelle began to run to Arnie at the water's edge. The party and everyone she knew was behind her. She couldn't run fast. She was pregnant and wearing flip flops and a long Hawaiian dress. But she lifted the edge of her skirt and she ran. He was laughing and so was she. She ran toward her love.

When she reached the water's edge, he faded away like a mirage in the desert. She spun around urgently, calling his name. *Arnie. Where are you? I just saw you. You motioned me to you. Don't play games with me now. Where are you?*

Arnie was no longer in view. But he was there. She could feel him. When she closed her eyes she could see him. She reached into her pocket again, to the bag with the ashes, and she could touch him. They were together in this place.

Isabelle began to sob as she waded out into the water. She didn't stop where she did for Arnie's eulogy with Grace. She kept going, deeper into the water, as if she were swimming out to a meet a wave – only she didn't have a surfboard. Snapshots of her life with Arnie pasted themselves randomly in her mind almost like a decoupage arrangement of memories, both good and not-so-good, they had created together over the last ten years.

Oh my gosh, what am I doing? Isabelle was struck by a distinct moment of clarity. *I came here tonight for a purpose. Not to get lost in the water.* Isabelle swam back toward the shore, and stopped in waist-deep water. She regained her footing and could stand on her own two feet again.

I'm sorry, Arnie. I'm sorry that I let you down. I'm sorry we let each other down. I'm sad without you, but I'm not broken. There are times I thought I wouldn't have picked you, I wouldn't have married you, if I had to do it over again. But I was wrong. It wasn't always easy, but I'm glad I picked you. I'm glad we married and created our family. I'm sorry I wasn't always the most aware partner. I miss you every day. I forgive you and I hope wherever you are, that you forgive me. I love you. And I love that you loved me.

Isabelle hung her head in raw sorrow and gasping pain. As she turned and walked toward the water's edge from the ocean, she fell and got caught in the shore break. All at once, it was as if an arm came out of the sky and pulled her arm up helping her to stand. She looked back. *Who's there?* She didn't see anyone. She kept walking.

Waiting for her on the sand was Harriet. *Oh dear, God. What is she going to say?* Harriet didn't say a word. She simply took Isabelle in her arms and let her cry. When Harriet finally spoke, the only words she had to say took Isabelle by surprise. "It's hard now, but you're going to be okay. And I'm going to be here to make sure of it."

Isabelle looked at her aunt and nodded.

Harriet smiled kindly. "There was a reason the good Lord kept me around. Now let's go get you cleaned up."

The next day, there were no guests at Zach and Amone's wedding. Everyone in attendance was part of the wedding party. It didn't matter that the numbers were untraditional with Robert being the only other man, aside from the groom, and the pastor from Lahaina Baptist Church, which Harriet faithfully attended when she was in Maui.

Amone had a bridesmaid in Carrie and two widowed matrons of honor with Isabelle and Harriet, and two flower girls, Grace and Pinky.

For decorations, they all wore traditional leis. Grace and Pinky had drawn a large heart in the sand and inside wrote, "Zach + Amone. March 23."

The ceremony was simple and traditional, except for the fact that it took place on a beach and not in a church, as Harriet pointed out, more than once. They were originally planning to get married in the little, white church with a tall steeple on the road to Hana, but either the Kaulanapueo Church got overbooked or somehow a glitch occurred. Three weeks before their trip, there were a lot of apologies from the volunteer staff there. It was fine. The bride and groom took this inconsequential turn in stride.

Zach and Amone had discussed writing their own vows, but that was another story. When Zach first agreed to do this, he intended for Isabelle to write his vows – which went over like a lead balloon with both Amone and Isabelle when he shared his idea with the girls.

Amone quickly conceded that traditional vows would be fine so long as he agreed to a wedding day toast to his bride. Amone was mature enough to know which battles were worth picking, and she knew this one was not.

Following the ceremony on the same beach where just a few days prior they celebrated the life of their friend and brother-in-law, the group made their way to the Sands of Kahana restaurant, where Zach had Amone's favorite Treveri sparkling wine chilled, along with cider for Isabelle and the two girls.

As promised, after the food was ordered, Zach stood to make a toast to Amone. "Please join me in toasting this amazing, gorgeous, patient, funny, unimaginably forgiving and loving woman who gave me the greatest gift today by becoming my wife. Amone, there are a few things I want to say to you today. First, I am neither as eloquent nor as long-winded as my sister, so you will know she did not write this toast." Everyone laughed, even Isabelle.

"Second, from the moment I carried our dog down that crazy steep hiking trail, I knew I was going to marry you. It might have taken us years to get together, but I knew the moment we met this day would come. I wasn't sure it would come in this lifetime or in anything beyond my own dreams and imagination, but I knew it could only be you.

"Third, it's been pointed out to me more than once that it took me a while to settle down. I don't have a problem with that because I never wanted to settle. No one seemed right until you came into my life. And it's not just because you're hot, although you are. You also let me be me, and you only give me that look when I already know I've pushed things a bit far. I kinda like the way you keep me in line. Keep doing that." Zach winked at his bride. Amone blushed.

"And finally, while I might not initiate deep conversations about the meaning of life, be rest assured, no one could love you more. I am absolutely the luckiest dude alive." Zach raised his glass to conclude his sincere if not slightly clumsy speech. "To Amone and a lifetime of good lovin'." Zach said as the family raised their glasses to toast in unison.

Although it wasn't intended to be funny, Zach just naturally was. Everyone broke out into laughter when he finished.

"That was absolutely the best, terrible toast I've ever heard," Isabelle said as she clapped her hands and laughed in approval.

"I wanted to conclude while the champagne was still chilled," Zach playfully fired back at his sister.

"I loved it," Amone said. "Thank you, Zach. I love you. To us and our amazing family," Amone added as she raised her glass.

"To marriage and everything it stands for, and everything unexpected it brings," Harriet said. "I feel grateful to be here with all of you today. I lived to see a seismic transformation in our family the last few months. Isabelle, Zach, I am so proud of you both. I am proud of us all, actually. Zach, I am honored to have been a part of raising Isabelle and you. What started out as my gift to Joy, in every way, became her gift to me. You are both the promise of hope that goodness wipes away the shadow of pain. Zach, you have found and married the perfect partner for you, a woman who cannot only handle you, but also challenges you. I know you could not be in any better hands with anyone than you are with Amone. To the son I love and Amone, the magnificent wife he very smartly chose to be his partner in life and my amazing daughter-in-law." Harriet raised her glass, sighed and paused to signal she was finished and the others could continue the toast.

"To my incredible friends who are family to me and always will be," Carrie said.

"To family and the blessings that come from making the effort. To Zach and Amone," Robert said.

"To Zach and Amone," the wedding party said in unison, followed by an unexpected echo of the same sentiments from other patrons in the quaint restaurant, who were also toasting the bride and groom. Isabelle looked around at the tiki torches that lined the swimming pool and mock grass roof on the bar. *There couldn't be a more perfect place to start a new life together.*

"I'm starving. Are we eating soon?" Grace asked. Just then, the server walked in with a huge tray of tropical, brightly-colored plates of food.

"Wait, wait. We almost forgot!" Isabelle shouted over the buzz.

Everyone stopped, startled by the unexpected interruption.

"We need a picture," Isabelle exclaimed. "Of the reception, we need a picture of the wedding party." Everyone gathered around the bride and groom – each with their champagne or cider toasting glass in hand.

Even the bartender took the liberty of dressing Grace and Pinky's glass with umbrellas and fruit garnish, which made them feel very grown up. Isabelle handed the server her phone to capture the moment. Everyone raised their glass toward the server doubling as a makeshift wedding photographer.

The picture captured more than the moment as it stood. It captured the love, the warmth, the trust, and the perseverance they shared. It captured the spirit of all they had been through together. It was much more than a toast to the couple. It was a toast to a family – a celebration of all their lives – and the promises they made to each other.